TO T

Nick Warburton was a primary school

In memory of
Jack Warburton and Bill Gittens

Nick Warburton would like to thank the
Eastern Arts Association and the Tyrone Guthrie
Centre at Annaghmakerrig, County Monaghan,
for their support.

First published 1994 by Walker Books Ltd
87 Vauxhall Walk, London SE11 5HJ

This edition published 1995

2 4 6 8 10 9 7 5 3 1

This book has been typeset in Sabon.

Printed in England

British Library Cataloguing in Publication Data
A catalogue record for this book is available from
the British Library.

ISBN 0-7445-3692-8

TO TRUST
A SOLDIER

NICK WARBURTON

WALKER BOOKS
AND SUBSIDIARIES
LONDON · BOSTON · SYDNEY

CHAPTER ONE

MARY:

The morning they first appeared at the farm I was standing by the well. I looked down the slope and thought, a peaceful morning settling on a peaceful land. I don't know how I could've been so foolish, or so forgetful.

I'd just unhooked the first bucket from the chain – it was heavy with cold water – and set it down on the flagstones. This is Old Jonah's task, I thought. He ought to be doing this. If I crank up many more buckets like this I'll end up with arms like his: thick, with muscles hard as branches. (Jonah always kept his sleeves rolled above the elbow, even on frosty mornings.) Then I remembered. Old Jonah wasn't around any more. It was funny how it caught me.

Anyway, the second bucket, being empty, picked up easily, as if it had no weight at all. I lifted it onto the wall of the well and I was just resting for a second when I saw a twinge of movement down the hill where there should've been none. A dark smudge, moving. I could easily have missed it altogether.

It was two fields away, down the slope where the old power machine, the tractor, had rusted into the hedgerow. A bit of the old twentieth century, forgotten and tangled up with the blackthorn so you could hardly tell plant from metal. I'd often caught sight of that old machine and pictured it moving by itself across the fields, like it must've done long before I was born. The thought always made me shudder.

And there was this dark smudge moving against the hedge.

It has, I thought. It's come to life.

Of course it wasn't that. Machines didn't move any more; I knew they didn't. My second thought was that maybe it was one of the cows. But the movement was too nimble for cows, and anyway I knew the cows were all in the upper meadow. So I shielded my eyes and looked closer. The sun was slanting straight at me by then.

The smudge took on human shape. And there were others; men, about half a dozen moving in a line, skirting the field towards the corner. And my heart set up such a pounding that I could hear it in my own ears.

I knew that when they reached the corner they'd find that little wooden gate, and they'd either disappear over it, or turn and follow the line of the field. Up the hill towards the farm.

Let them climb over, I said to myself. I was watching so closely I think I said it out loud, in a kind of whisper. Let them go away again, right out of sight.

When they got to the corner they stopped. They didn't look as if they knew where they really wanted to go, those tiny figures. They hung around, like they were waiting for some kind of inspiration. And I stood, solid as stone, watching them. I picked out the diagonal lines of white straps against brown tunics. And packs and rolls all neat at their shoulders.

God save us, I said to myself. They're soldiers. God save us all.

That little rhyme came into my head and went round and round while I stood there:

The Vixen from over the waters;
She'll eat your sons and daughters.

Just those couple of lines, over and over. They sounded quaint, like a game you'd play to make the little ones laugh. But I wasn't laughing then. Those silly words had so filled me with fear that I could not move.

The Vixen from over the waters...
The Vixen from over the waters...

* * *

7

Six men are strung out in an irregular line. Three of them quite young. Each with a pack and a rifle.

They are tired. They have been marching through the night with little idea of where they are. The long grass round the edge of the field sweeps whispers of frost over their legs. Sometimes it knots across their feet and causes them to fall. Or turn an ankle on a frozen rut, throw out an arm and tumble silently.

The way across the middle of the field provides easier walking but the sergeant has told them to stick to the edge where the grass is long. It is always a mistake to tramp across the middle of strange fields for all the world to see, he says. And better to march at night, too, he says: rest and hide during the day.

When they come to the little gate at the corner of the field, they stop and take the chance to rest. They wait for the sergeant to catch them up. If they have a choice about which path to take the sergeant makes it for them. When he arrives, he stares hard at the gate for a moment or two; then turns and glances up the hill. He narrows his eyes, sees something – a tiny flash in the morning sun – and decides.

The soldiers pull themselves to their feet and begin to move again. They turn their backs on the gate and follow the hedge up the slope, towards the brow of the hill.

As they move, one of the young soldiers wipes a palm against his tunic and feels the hard disc of a coin in his breast pocket. He slips it out and, without looking down, squeezes it for luck.

He knows that on one side it is stamped with the image of a woman with a crown, and that her name is marked round the edge. Not the name they call her in England: in England they call her the Vixen.

A coin in a soldier's pocket.

A face stamped in metal. The hard, fixed gaze of a woman who might be standing on a shore somewhere and staring across the sea. Staring, unblinking. Setting her face like the sergeant sets his: into the wind.

MARY:

At that moment, when they turned and started up the slope towards me, my fortune turned too. It turned like a cart does in the middle of a busy street: everything gets swept round by it.

I looked round and saw the bucket, still balanced on the well with the sun striking it, and I snatched it off and set it down on the stones. It rang out like a high, cracked bell and the sound of it went clashing through the cold air. I lugged up the full one and struggled back to the yard, thinking to myself that I'd been a proper fool. That I'd been soft-headed to hope the Vixen's soldiers would never come this way.

I was heading for the house when I realized that that was another mistake. The soldiers would make straight for the house – they were bound to.

9

So I veered round and went towards the cowshed. I was still lugging that bucket, slopping water over my feet, everywhere, and too scared to think of putting the thing down. And I could hear this harsh whispering, over and over, running through my head. My own voice.

God save us all. God save us from the Vixen.

I stopped inside the shed and took a breath. I don't think I'd had a gasp of air all the way across the yard. There was a kind of close greyness in that shed. Almost comforting. It was a relief to breathe the sweet cow smell and to be out of the sunlight. I put the bucket down behind the door and thought to myself, Oh, Mary, why did you make such a mindless prayer?

God save us all? He had no need to save us all. The farm had been empty for nearly three days. The Campions had gone. Little Lizzie, my charge. Even Old Jonah, who'd worked on the farm so long he could remember the days of the old power machines, before horses. All gone.

All I could recall of the day they left was rushing through the wood at the back of the house. Rushing to fetch the doll Lizzie had left there. Then falling. And waking to find the wood empty, the farm deserted.

So now there was only me to be saved, and the Vixen had sent her soldiers at last. They'd crossed the water and were in our land.

To eat our sons and daughters...

I bit the back of my hand to stop myself crying.

I was all alone. Maybe the Campions thought I'd rushed on ahead. Maybe God thought that too. Maybe not even He knew I was here.

It was quiet for a while. For ages, it felt.

I was wishing the cows would walk in from the upper meadow and join me in the shed. So I could hide behind their solid, warm flanks while they gave me those backward glances that they do with their gentle eyes. It would've been some comfort. But now all I had of them was their smell in the straw, dark and sweet.

I'd never had much to do with them before. Cows were cows, it seemed to me; all more or less the same. Since I'd had the farm to myself, though, I'd come to think differently of them; think of them more as companions.

There was a big, black one with a mild, white face; usually last out of the meadow when I brought them in. I called her Campion, after my master's family. It sounds disrespectful, I know, to give the name to a slow old cow. But I didn't mean it like that. I loved that cow.

I sat still, listening for soldiers. There was nothing else I could do.

CHAPTER TWO

When they reach the brow of the hill, the soldiers find a well with a pitched roof. Beyond it are whitewashed walls, about as high as a man's shoulder, skirting a number of farm buildings. But no sign of life.

The sergeant sends two men to investigate the rear of the premises; the young soldier with the lucky coin and an older man. They set off at a kind of stooping run, keeping their heads below the level of the wall. Round the back of the house the wall turns into a hedge. On the other side of the hedge is a wood. The two soldiers look at each other. A wood like that, with its trees and its shadows, might hide more men than they can count.

They see some sort of hen-house in a scrap of garden so they lurk around there. They keep their rifles trained on the back of the house, but half their attention is fixed on the wood.

After three or four minutes they hear the

sergeant call them from the house. The young soldier jumps at the sound of his voice. His finger twitches on the trigger of his rifle but he manages not to fire.

The whole place is empty. It has that look about it. Once they are inside the house they can sense that it's empty.

The relief they feel at this is so great that they run from room to room, flinging open doors, jumping on beds. Some of them laugh. One hurls open a pair of windows in one of the upstairs rooms and bellows out, loud, across the fields till the sergeant appears behind him and silences him. One word from the sergeant is enough.

They go down to the kitchen and find three eggs on a dresser. A tall young man, with flaxen hair that flops over his forehead, picks up one of the eggs and lets it fall on the kitchen floor. They stand there quietly for a moment, watching the thin shell roll aside and the yoke spread and run.

MARY:

First there were the sounds of feet hurrying across the yard, heavy and urgent. But no voices. I huddled there in my drift of straw and closed my eyes. There was nothing for a while, and then shouting from inside the house. And laughter. All indistinct and kind of jagged off the stone walls. Then I realized it would've done me no good to make out the words anyway: I wouldn't have understood them.

That was a strange feeling. A group of soldiers

13

jabbering away in their own tongue while I, who spoke the King's proper English, had to keep my mouth shut. It was like the world had turned upside down: I was the foreigner and they were at home.

A window was thrown open. One of the upper windows at the east end by the sound of it. It slammed and shook against the wall and a man's voice cried out. It was a weird, high, yodelling cry which sprang off the stable wall and thinned out over the fields. And it caused my arms and legs to start shaking. That cry frightened me even more than the first sight of the soldiers, I think. It was so savage.

I tried to make sounds fit the pictures I held in my head. Those tiny brown figures, high-stepping through the long grass, heads down, rifles waving before them thin as stalks. I couldn't make the two things match. But there was no mistaking it: they were there all right, full-sized and loud, and in the farmhouse that had been mine alone for the past three days. The Vixen's men, turning our land into hers.

Well, I couldn't stay shivering in the cowshed, so I asked myself what I intended to do. With the soldiers stuck in the house I could take my chance and slip away. But where? Down the valley to Terston? Out in the countryside? In open fields where I might run into other roaming packs of men?

I thought and thought but kept coming back to the same answer. To go away was the greater risk. Stay where you are, on the farm. There was nowhere else. I could find a better hiding-place than the cowshed. The stables, perhaps, where there was a hayloft. Then keep out of sight and wait.

They were soldiers. They wouldn't stay long.

I waited a while before I could bring myself to get up. When I did, there was such a pain of stiffness down my right side that I couldn't stand straight and had to hold on to the wall. It scared me that I might fall over and make a noise. Eventually, though, I got to the door and looked out. The house was still but not empty. It didn't have that empty look about it. And I caught sight of some dark figures in one of the kitchen windows, just standing there with their heads bowed, peering at something. It looked strange, like a prayer meeting.

The stables were directly opposite the cowshed. I could run it in five or six seconds but I knew that it would be far safer to go the long way round. Out at the yard gates and round by the white wall. Then climb back over the wall and get in by the loose boards Old Jonah had been meaning to fix for the last few weeks.

Go now, then, I told myself.

So I stepped out into the light.

And I heard the click of the latch across the yard. One of the soldiers, dipping his head and shoulders, was coming out of the kitchen door.

I froze where I stood. I yearned to shrink back into the shadows but I knew I couldn't do that. Any movement, even the lifting of my arm, might make him look my way.

He straightened up again and I saw his face. He was young, maybe no more than a year or two older than me, and he was tall and awkward. He didn't look like a soldier. I thought he was going to stand there gawping round till he had to see me, but he suddenly turned away and set off along the side of the house towards the garden at the back.

As he turned the corner, I heard him begin to whistle.

A soldier with a round face and thinning hair stands in the dining-room. He hooks a pair of glasses over his ears and peers crookedly at a shelf of books. After a moment he looks round and sees some writing-paper on a low table. He picks it up and begins to make notes with a stub of pencil he's found in the kitchen.

Following instructions. Note down anything that can be used, the sergeant said. Anything that might help.

There isn't much. He sees pale squares on the walls where pictures have been removed; an old candlestick at one end of an otherwise empty shelf; a wooden box on its side, spilling some balls of wool across a rush mat. Most of it not worth noting.

The man moves slowly round the room. He puts his boot against a chair and pushes it aside. There are some pegs on the floor, bound together with wool to make a child's doll. He takes it up and looks at it for a second. Then, tossing it onto the empty fire, he returns to the shelves.

Perhaps he'll find a map tucked in among the books. They are lost in countryside which might be hiding all manner of dangers. A map will be even more use to them than food.

MARY:
The hayloft above the stables felt more of a home than the cowshed. Because it was off the ground it felt safer.

Home, I thought. Yes. This'll be my home now. Till the soldiers have gone.

The loft had a small square window at one end and through this I could see the house. I was almost on a level with the attic I had shared with Bridget. I had never had the run of the place – Bridget was always in charge – but I had had one corner of it, where my bed was tucked under the sloping ceiling and where I kept my decorated tin and my prayer book on a box covered with a blue cloth. It seemed an age ago now.

These things were running through my head when I heard the click of feet below. Someone was walking by. Then they stopped. By standing on tip-toe I could look down on the top of his head.

An older man this time. He had thin, sandy hair and he was relighting a pipe. Being so high above him, and out of sight, gave me a feeling of power.

I could drop something on him, I thought. If I had a sack of seed or a farrier's hammer, I could watch it spinning down on his skull.

17

Then he'd buckle all right. It might even kill him.

The thought surprised me. It would be murder.

But could you call it murder if they'd come to take over your country, to burn and kill?

Maybe it was my duty.

I looked round the loft for some object to snatch up. Then I heard another sound. The kitchen door had opened and when I looked down again another man was there. A man with a hard, lined face; the way I imagined soldiers really looked. This man spoke.

He said: "Have you got me that list yet, Jack?"

In English.

CHAPTER THREE

MARY:

After I'd heard that soldier speak I didn't know what to do. The words had been small and distant but they'd floated up to me as clear as anything. Our words. Not foreign. These weren't the Vixen's men at all. I crawled back into the darkest corner of the loft, and curled myself up to turn it all over in my mind.

These were my own people, then, and yet I could not feel safe. There was something about them that made them not my own, either. They weren't like anyone else I knew. Not Mr Campion, or Roger or Jonah. I'd only seen three of them close to. The youth who whistled, the one who stopped to light his pipe, and the one who'd spoken. And it was him, that last one, who caused me most trouble. That soldier's face of his, blank and hard as a wall. And the flat way he spoke, without any feeling.

I tried to imagine what it would be like to go

down there and speak to them. How I might lift the latch on the kitchen door and see the look of surprise as they turned to me.

My name is Mary. I live here.

But all I could picture was his hard face, and there was no answering comfort in that. So I did nothing. The hayloft remained my home and for two more days and nights I stayed where I was.

I grew very hungry and the hunger was at its worst in the deepest, coldest part of the night. It got so bad, that first night, that I was driven to go in search of food.

I could see the dark house from my little window. There was an edge of silver on the roof from a high moon. Everything was still and quiet and I guessed the men were all inside, probably in the kitchen, so I made my way into the garden and filled my apron with chicken-feed from the sack in the shed. By chance my fingers also came across an egg.

I was stretching out to feel for more when I heard the gravel crunch. Not twenty paces from where I crouched. And a soft, tuneless whistling. Both sounds, the whistling and the gravel, were coming towards me. Then I made out a shape emerging from the shadow of the house. It slowed and hesitated. I held my breath. The whistling stopped and I prepared to run. Straight for the hedge if need be and into the wood.

The figure took another step forward and a hard line of moonlight marked the top of a head. There

20

were deep shadows in place of eyes, but I was sure he was looking at me. Then his arm moved. A flicker of pale light.

His hand.

His rifle. He's reaching for his rifle.

My muscles tightened but I didn't move.

The hand stopped moving. It flattened itself against his chest. And he seemed to be waiting.

HOBBS:

I was on watch, shuffling round the outside of the house, my head full of thoughts about nothing, and I saw this face. God save us, the sight was enough to flatten me. I stopped where I was and put my hand on my heart, it was thumping so much.

A round shape low down in the garden, where you'd never expect a face to be. For half a moment it didn't look that out of place. It was like turning your head and catching sight of a rose. But this wasn't a rose. It was no kind of flower at all, but a creamy-white face in a dark garden.

The thought that it was the enemy never occurred to me. No. My head was filled with things like sprites and fairy folk – for this was the face of a child.

I only saw it for a second. I glanced, and saw a flower, and then the flower became a face. Then it was gone.

It was never there, I told myself. You made it up out of your own imaginings. But I noticed I still had my hand against my heart. Between my fingers and my heart was my lucky coin. And that made me feel a bit better.

I don't know why I call it lucky. I can't recall it doing much for me: it didn't prevent us getting lost. And, of course, it has the Vixen's face on it, so by rights it should be unlucky; a little piece of the enemy. It was palmed off on me in the shop one afternoon; palmed off as one of our own, true coins. I looked down, I remember, and I thought, heck, the king looks young on this. Then I looked a bit closer and saw it was a woman. Bloody hell, I said to myself, it's the Vixen. What a nerve – spending the Vixen's coins in our shop for proper goods. I daren't tell the old man. He'd've skinned me. I had to make it up with a real coin from my own savings. I would've chucked it away but I thought, no, it's yours. Hang on to it. It might bring a spot of luck. A fair distant hope, it seemed just then.

Anyway, I circled the house once more with my ears pricked for the slightest sound. What I'd taken for a quiet night was now full of noises. None of them very great but half of them weird enough to turn your hair white. Rustling and scurryings and screeches from the trees.

When I passed the kitchen door I considered going inside to report the incident.

All quiet, Hobbs?

All quiet, sergeant. Except for a fairy face in the garden.

I didn't waste long over that idea. I could just

22

see the lot of them laughing me back outside.

When I'd circled back round to the garden I gathered up enough courage to take a proper look. I went stepping over plants and shadows with my rifle ready to blast whatever budged.

But nothing did budge.

You've been sleeping in too many strange places, I told myself. Your mind's not all it should be at present. All the same, I was heartily glad when Webby came out to take over from me.

MARY:
He paused. Waited. The whistling began again, soft and uncertain. Then the footsteps started up, the whistling faded away, and I could move.

My meal that night was a paste of chicken-feed and raw egg, and even though my stomach felt light from the shock of nearly being discovered, I was hungry enough to find it very good. As good as any of the cakes Bridget used to bake on Friday afternoons.

After that I became a spy.

I watched those soldiers and learned what I could about them. There was little else to do up in the loft.

They kept themselves busy. There was always something going on. To-ing and fro-ing across the yard. At times I was almost tricked into thinking the farm was back to normal; that Mrs Campion, or Bridget, or Susan might come out of the kitchen and exchange a friendly word with one of the men.

Almost that I might see Lizzie skipping by on some expedition she'd dreamed up. All those thoughts disappeared, though, whenever I caught sight of the one they called Talbot, the sergeant. He was such a dark-looking soul. I knew him now to be one of our own men, one of those risking his life to defend us, but he might've been the worst that the Vixen could throw at us for all the difference it made.

It muddled me up. I'd been expecting the enemy. I knew now that these were our men, but I still felt afraid.

So all the time that I watched them in secret, I was praying for them to leave. Trying, through the force of will, to make them pack their gear and go.

On the third day they did leave. But it didn't happen the way I'd willed it. There was no joy in their going. No joy at all.

I woke up and heard shouting in the distance. In fact I think I'd heard the shouting for several moments before I was awake. There were voices shouting, not at each other but together, screaming on one long note. Then silence for a bit. Then the shouting again. I opened my eyes and saw a dusty shaft of sunlight coming from the small window. I sat up and pulled some stalks of hay from my hair.

I'd got used to them making a noise about the place, but not with any pattern to it. And there was pattern to this. A yell, then silence; a yell, then silence. It puzzled me. I went over to the window

24

to see what was going on. The noise was away to the left somewhere, beyond the gates. I couldn't see over there from my window. If I wanted to see, I'd have to go down the ladder and put my nose out at the stable door.

Well, I felt fortune had already blessed me when I escaped after finding the egg, but I didn't want to risk it again. Not in broad daylight. Curiosity wasn't enough to get me out of hiding.

Then I saw one of them come out of the kitchen and turn east, heading up towards the high lane. He was the quietest, hardly ever said a word, and he was plump and round-faced; one of the three lads. They called him Webby but his name was Webster, I think. He had an apple in his hand and his rifle over his shoulder. The sight of that apple set my hunger off again. I could still remember the taste of the egg and chicken feed; how good it had been.

I concentrated on the shouting for a while and tried to count the voices. I thought there were three. Maybe more.

Perhaps it would be worth the risk. If there was no one in the kitchen … I could imagine those apples in the pantry, in a basket next to cool, round cheeses.

So I trod quickly and steadily down the ladder. It was a right uncomfortable feeling, with my back to the open, and I was glad when my foot touched the brick floor. I looked out of the stable door and saw nothing. Just the gates and, beyond them, the field dipping into the shallow valley. It all looked so calm. Then I heard another long, wavery shout and saw heads appearing above the rise. It was an odd sight: these heads with gaping mouths bobbing up like they were suddenly growing out of the ground. Three, four of them. Then their shoulders, jogging from side to side, and their rifles held out in front of them. Blades flashed at the ends of the rifles. They looked as if they were coming straight for me, then they veered off to the right, still shouting, and disappeared behind the thorn bushes.

The shouting stopped and I heard the sergeant's voice barking out, still behind the rise. So there were five out there in the field. And Webster on his way to the lane. All accounted for.

Well, I thought, as long as the sergeant keeps giving orders, I should be safe.

HOBBS:
You felt you were a kid again, clattering up that hill and yelling your lungs out. Mind you, we were all doing it, even Farrar and Crowe, who were getting on in years, so you didn't feel too much of a pudger. And it was training, I suppose.

Talbot kept us at it. We'd labour up the slope, swing left and drop to the ground. Then you had to make firing noises, go through the motions of reloading and make another lot of firing noises. I can tell you, you got so short of breath at times that your firing sounded more like a fart!

And there was Talbot, calm as you like, waiting

to give us his opinion of our efforts.

"Fling yourself down, Hobbs! You're not stretching out for a nap. And, Crowe, look where you're going, man. You just shot Farrar up the arse!"

Then it was back down the hill and start again.

We must've done it about a dozen times when I flung myself down, as directed, and trapped my thumb under the trigger guard. God, it hurt, and blood started oozing out and I thought, that's it; you've been wounded in action.

"You daft turnip," Talbot bellowed. "You're dripping all over your uniform. Get back to the farm and wrap something round it."

MARY:
There was honey on the kitchen table, some scattered crusts and a block of butter. I snatched up a cloth and began to pile things into it. Not too much; I didn't want to let them know I'd been there. Just what the men might've taken as they wandered past.

Every time the shouting stopped I stopped too, and held myself still till it started again. I think it was that, concentrating so hard on the sounds coming from the distance, that made me almost miss a much lighter noise only just outside. The scuffing of boots on flagstones. Someone coming.

I swung the cloth off the table and by the time the latch clicked I was in the dining-room, standing behind the door and trying to keep my breathing quiet. Through the crack I saw the whistling soldier at the kitchen table. The one called Hobbs.

This is the third time I've all but run into you, I thought. And again I felt a little lucky. He never seemed to notice things. Some of the others would've sensed that there was someone watching them.

He was holding his hand up to his face and there was blood trickling down his fingers. The house had fallen so quiet now that I could hear the soft pit-pit of several drops hitting the floor. He sucked at his thumb and began to pull open drawers with his other hand. Then he moved out of sight, somewhere towards the pantry.

I tiptoed through the dining-room to the window at the back of the house. It was a wide window with a deep sill and it overlooked the garden. I knew it squeaked if you pulled it open so I eased it as gently as I could. It moaned: wood rubbing on wood.

There was no sound from the kitchen. He might've been standing there, alert and listening. Or maybe just seeing to his hand, tugging on a bit of linen with his teeth.

Then I realized. There was no other sound either. The shouting had stopped.

I pulled at the window again. It came open easily and without any more noise. I climbed onto the sill and lowered my feet onto the gravel path outside.

"Hobbs," I heard someone call. "Hobbs."

The kitchen was suddenly crowded with voices.

And chairs being scraped and heavy objects being dumped on the table and the floor.

I remembered running along that path only a week before; before I knew anything about spying and soldiers. Then I'd ground my feet deliberately into the gravel because I liked the sound it made. Now I was fearful and stepped off the path, onto the patch of earth Roger had been digging for potatoes. I went nimbly in and out of shrubs towards the corner of the house. The nearer I got, the safer I felt. And I still had my prize, the cloth full of food, clutched to my chest.

Once round the corner the path broadened along a stretch of wall that had no windows in it. I felt free to run and that's what I did, straight and hard. Ahead of me I could see the arch of poles framed by waving wands of forsythia. Like a golden gate. And beyond the arch were the stables. Home.

Then, suddenly, I couldn't see the stables any more.

The arch was blocked.

When I understood why, it was too late.

I couldn't stop running. Running, running.

Straight into the bulk of a soldier.

HOBBS:

One moment I was looking at my thumb with Farrar and Crowe peering over each shoulder, and the next the place was full of the sounds of screaming and thumping. To be honest there was just

29

one scream, then a fair amount of shouting from Kerridge outside. The three of us looked at each other, with my thumb still stuck in the air for inspection.

"What the hell's going on out there?" said Farrar, and we all went out to see.

It was a good deal more than we were expecting. It was Kerridge with a girl pinned against the wall. He had her by both wrists and he was leaning against her, pushing his face close to hers.

"Now then, now then," he was saying. "And where did you spring from?"

She'd twisted her face away from him and she wasn't answering. There was a cloth at their feet and lumps of cheese and bread had gone bouncing onto the path. It looked to me as if Kerridge was being a bit too rough and ready with her. Enjoying himself more than he ought to've done, too.

"Look what I've found," he grinned round at us. "Snooping about round the back of the house."

"Very nice," said Farrar. "Let's have a proper look, then."

He had his hands in his pockets, as if he was a farmer at a market or something. Kerridge jerked the girl's head round to face us.

My God, it fell into place then all right.

That face: I'd seen it before. It stunned me so much I couldn't speak. Which was just as well because I don't know what I could've said that wouldn't have sounded right foolish.

"Ease up a bit," Crowe said. "Let's take her

inside and see what the sergeant has to say."

I dragged my heels a bit, still feeling the effects of the shock. I noticed this chicken picking its way through the garden; darting its head about and stabbing at the bread like nothing much had happened at all.

MARY:

I was right to fear them. I'd been right to hide. Maybe they weren't the Vixen's men but they weren't much like humankind either.

They sat me in the kitchen. It was my kitchen more than theirs, but sitting there with them all looking at me made it all feel unfamiliar. All the objects I knew so well looked odd and out of place.

One of the older men, Mr Crowe, put a mug of tea in front of me. I wrapped my hands round it and stared at the table. I didn't want to see any of them. Didn't even want to catch sight of them.

"Manners," said a voice. "You've just been given tea. What do you say?"

"There's no need for that," Mr Crowe said.

"What do you mean?"

"She's only a kid, Kerridge. Fifteen at most."

"Well?"

"Can't you see she's frightened?"

"So she bloody well should be. Creeping around stealing things."

"It's no more than we've done," came a quiet voice behind me.

I knew it was Hobbs though I couldn't see him.

31

He spoke as if he didn't really want anyone to hear him.

The sergeant had said not a word so far. He sat on the edge of the table with his arms folded, staring at me. However much I tried not to look I couldn't help noticing him out of the corner of my eye. When Hobbs spoke he shifted his position, arms still folded, and glanced at him. I saw all this even with my eyes down. I took it all in, as if these were my last moments on earth.

"Where's she come from?" someone was saying. "That's what we've got to find out."

"She can't've come far, not dressed like that."

"I mean what's she up to? You have to be careful."

"She's working for the Vixen, then, is she?" Mr Crowe asked with a kind of laugh.

"She might be."

"Don't be ridiculous. You only have to look at her."

"Yes, but they use kids, don't they? Especially girls. They said that at the camp…"

And that's when the sergeant decided it was time for him to speak.

"That'll do," he said. "I'll talk to her myself."

"But, Sarge…"

"That'll do. If there are questions to ask, Kerridge, I'll ask them. You can go out and relieve Webster. And you, Farrar."

He sent the other two packing as well, so I was alone with him.

He dragged a chair up close and straddled it with his arms resting on the back. He'd set it so that he could see me but I couldn't see him properly without turning my head. His face was just a blur: thick eyebrows and the shadow of a long nose. That was all right, though. I didn't want to see him. I looked up and fixed my eyes on the dresser, and I stiffened myself inside. I was determined he shouldn't make me weep.

"What's your name?" he said after a pause.

"Mary."

"And what are you doing here?"

"I was hungry…"

"Yes?"

"I was just passing by. I saw the house and I thought…"

"Where were you when you saw it?"

"Down the hill. That way."

"Didn't you see us? We were in the field."

"I did, yes. I kept to the other side of the hedge."

"So you took some food?" he said softly. "And that's all you wanted?"

It wasn't a proper question so I didn't say anything.

"It's a strange thing for a girl like yourself to be wandering the countryside alone. Didn't you run into anyone else?"

"No, sir."

"That was lucky for you. There's two big armies out there somewhere. Thousands of men. You know about that?"

"Yes, sir."

I could hear the breath in his nostrils, slow and deliberate.

"One of those armies is your enemy, Mary. That must be so. What I'm wondering, of course, is which?"

"I'm not a spy," I said.

But I said it before I realized it wasn't true. I was. I'd spent hours spying on them.

"But what am I to think? Here you are, wandering around by yourself."

"I was with my family but I got lost. It's easy to get lost round here."

Like you did, I thought.

He stood up and moved round in front of me. Then he leaned forward with his knuckles on the table. I couldn't avoid his face now. His eyes were flecked and blue, dull as washed cloth, with peppery skin round them and heavy lids.

"War is like a game," he said. "It has rules. One of them is that I have to decide what to do when slips of girls turn up out of nowhere. That's hard enough, but you're making it harder. We've been here for three days. And so have you."

"No, sir."

"Yes!"

He said it sharply, deliberately to make me jump.

"You were at the well when we arrived. I know you were," he said and gave a little nod at the back door. "I don't tell them but that's another rule. I have to keep some things to myself till the time is right. But I know you've been here all the time."

I had to concentrate hard not to cry. He had power over me. He could see inside my head and it made me confused. I didn't know what I should say any more.

"I have to make my mind up about you, girl, and we're off to a bad start because you've been telling me lies."

"I only…"

"You only what?"

"I only said I was passing by. That was the only lie. I live here really. I just got left behind when the others left."

He straightened up and gave a deep sigh. Then he went to the door and shouted into the yard for Hobbs.

"All right," he said, turning back to me. "I believe you. Just keep telling me the truth."

Hobbs appeared in the doorway almost at once. He couldn't have been far away.

"Find this girl something to eat," Mr Talbot told him. "And then keep an eye on her."

He didn't say another word, or give me another glance. He went striding out into the yard with a blank expression on his face.

HOBBS:

I set about cutting some bread but in no time at all it had all gone lopsided. I made two or three

35

attempts and they each of them went wrong. The girl said nothing when I put them in front of her, though.

It didn't please me to be left with her, to be honest. I knew she was real enough by this time, but I couldn't clear my head of that face in the garden. I suppose I'd've been nervous anyway, stuck in a kitchen with a girl and told to keep an eye on her. The thought of sprites and things just made it harder. But an order's an order, no matter what; and there'd've been hell and a half to pay if she'd upped and flitted out of a window. So I did keep an eye on her, but I managed to do it without really looking at her much.

Not that it mattered. She barely moved. Ate the bread, that's all.

Another thing to puzzle about was who she was. I didn't know. She must've been some sort of local. She wasn't a spy – any fool but Kerridge could see that. No, she probably lived around the place somewhere – that wasn't the puzzle – but what I couldn't fathom out was what she was to us. I mean, was I supposed to be taking care of her, or was she our prisoner?

From the look on Talbot's face when he first caught sight of her, I took it that she was a prisoner. His is a face that doesn't register much, but when Farrar and Kerridge marched her into the kitchen there was definitely a twitch of something on it. If you pressed me I'd've said it was disappointment. As if she'd spoiled something for him by turning up like that.

Anyway, there she sat, busy with the bread, till Talbot came back with Crowe and Webster in tow. I was glad to be in a kitchen of five instead of just with her. Not a word was said but they set their rifles on the table and started to clean them. Then, when Talbot did speak, he was unusually chatty. For him, anyway.

"Do you know the area well, Mary?" he said.

So that was her name. Funny: it had never occurred to me to ask. There was a Mary who used to come into the shop. A solid girl with heavy arms. Not like this one.

"Yes, sir," she said.

"How far?"

"All around here, sir. Twenty miles or more."

Well, I thought, this doesn't sound like the way you talk to prisoners so perhaps she isn't.

"You know a place called Black Garlock?" he went on.

"Yes. It's a good way off but I do know it."

Jack Crowe had been rubbing away at the rifle barrel and getting slower and slower. The mention of Black Garlock made him stop altogether. Old Jack fretted to be getting at the Vixen's army more than any of us. He didn't look at Talbot or the girl but you could tell he was listening. Even Webster seemed to be paying attention.

"You could take us there, then?" said Talbot.

"I could, but…"

"Good. Well, Jack," he said, "you can stop

searching for your map. It looks like we've got one here."

MARY:
When he asked me about Black Garlock the soldiers started to bustle about and there was something like excitement in their movements. They went off to call the others and get their gear ready. Mr Talbot sat close to me again.

"You understand what I'm saying?" he said. "We've got to get to this place and you're coming with us."

But I hadn't understood that much. It hadn't sunk in.

"You mean I'm to be your prisoner?"

"I wouldn't say that."

"But…"

"You can't stay here. It won't be safe for much longer. From now on I'll be your safe-keeping, Mary. And you'll be our map."

I had to swallow hard. For so long I'd waited for them to leave. I'd imagined it and hoped for it. But not like this. I never thought I'd be going with them.

He grabbed my face. The first time he'd touched me. He was squeezing my cheeks together, the way Granny used to, too hard sometimes. His hand was colder and firmer than Granny's, though, and rough as dry bark.

"One thing more, Mary," he said. "You do exactly as I say. You show *me* the way to Black Garlock, not them. Understand?"

He loosened his grip and I nodded.

"The rules of war, Mary. You must promise to keep them or it might be the death of us all."

He was quiet but fierce, too, and the fierceness frightened me. There was more to it than that, though. I wasn't just afraid of him. I also believed him. I believed that I had to do as he said or we might all die.

"I promise," I said.

CHAPTER FOUR

MARY:

We set off along the high lane towards the upper meadow. Mr Talbot led the way and he kept me close behind him. I could hear the crunch of boots at my back and Kerridge at the end of the line singing, as if we were going on a picnic. On the brow of the hill I stopped. Mr Talbot leaned on his rifle.

"What's the matter?" he asked.

I didn't answer. If he didn't know why I'd stopped there was no point telling him. And anyway, I couldn't've explained it in a steady voice.

"It's her home, Sergeant," Mr Crowe said, half turning his back to me. "She might not see it again."

And the sergeant shrugged and waited. I knew well enough what I could see of the house from that point and it wasn't much. Part of the east end roof and a corner of the stables. The tall oak in the garden. I remembered fixing a rope to that tree for

Lizzie to swing on.

"Is this it?" shouted Kerridge. "That didn't take long, then, did it?"

And he blundered up the slope, grinning. His thin face came between me and the farm. A hank of yellow hair flopped into his eyes. That's what they were like, those soldiers. They spoiled everything; sometimes because they meant to and sometimes because they were too stupid to know what they were about. I turned my back on the place, pushed past Mr Talbot and began to walk away. The incline quickened my steps and the others had to hurry to keep up.

The Campions had left and I was leaving too. I told myself the farmhouse would be truly deserted now, just a group of empty buildings that didn't mean anything. Don't think about it any more.

The track wound on into the countryside. We reached the little boulder with the painted arrow, where the path divided. The arrow was pointing back the way we'd come. No words with it. People who got this far knew it could only mean the Campions' place. If we turned left here it would take us over the stone bridge and up to the back of the woods. The men paused and looked at me. They didn't ask and I didn't answer. I just nodded to the right and we carried on.

Somewhere behind us the sun was a deep yellow; low and big in the sky. Kerridge and Mr Farrar kept up a conversation in low voices, and smirked and giggled. Mr Farrar was an older man, like Jack Crowe, but he didn't always act like one. From time to time Hobbs whistled to himself. No one said anything to me until the sergeant fell in beside me.

"Where is this taking us?" he said quietly.

"To the Motley Road."

"Then what?"

"We take that road west for a short way. Then go south…"

"Is that a right turn at the Motley Road?"

"Yes."

"How much further must we go before we reach it?"

"Three hours. I can't be sure."

"This Motley Road, it's a main route, I take it."

"Yes. It goes east to Motley itself."

"Then it's big enough for troops and artillery. We'll avoid it. Can you find your way over the fields?"

"I think so."

"Good. That's what we'll do, then."

I wasn't confident that I'd find my way to Black Garlock if we left the roads. There were landmarks to look out for – church spires, certain trees and so on – but I couldn't be sure I'd see them from the fields. Even if I managed it we'd have to cross the Motley Road at some point. I didn't let Mr Talbot know what I was thinking, though. What would he do if he thought I was no use to him? If we got lost?

We walked on and on. Sometimes they hesitated

where other tracks crossed ours, waiting for my directions. Then we came to a small stretch of wood. Some way into it was a clearing. I knew that well enough. Last September I'd taken Lizzie there to look for blackberries. The longest adventure she'd ever been on, she said. It was an oval-shaped space of long, pale grass. There were four silver birches at one end. They looked tall and elegant, almost like human figures against the squat, dark wood and the tangled fruit bushes.

By this time the sun had disappeared and the light was beginning to fade. Mr Talbot took us off the track and said we'd stop in the clearing for the night.

Hobbs and Mr Crowe set about treading the grass flat while the others unfolded their sleeping sacks and fiddled around with their gear. I heard some creature go rustling away into the under-growth. Night had reached the wood already and was hanging in the trees as if it belonged there. As the men settled themselves I had the feeling that the darkness was seeping out through trunks and branches to collect around them.

Nobody's land, I thought. Home to creatures, not men.

I sat apart from the others. I had no bedding roll but I'd brought my large, hooded cloak with me. Even though there was no real chill to the evening yet, I pulled it tight round my shoulders. Above the trees, out over the fields, a hawk was on its last gliding search of the day. I watched it dip below the treetops, then reappear to flicker its wings and fan its tail.

In a little while the soldiers became no more than mounds in the grass. Mr Crowe lit his pipe and leant on one elbow to peer closely at a book. Mr Talbot was sitting up with his back against one of the silver birches. I couldn't make out his face but I was sure he was wide awake and staring. Keeping an eye on me and the men. Perhaps he thought I'd try to slip away in the night. He needn't have worried. There was nowhere for me to go. I didn't like the thought of spending the next few days in their company, but there was nothing else I could do.

At least, I kept telling myself, they're the king's men. At least I'm not a prisoner of the Vixen.

I was beginning to drowse when a thump on the grass behind me made me open my eyes wide and turn round. Hobbs was standing over me, silhouetted against the deep blue of the sky.

"I just thought," he said, "you might get cold."

With his foot he tapped the sleeping sack he'd dropped.

"I've got my cloak," I said.

"Well, it's there if you want it. I don't feel the cold that much."

"I'll be all right."

He stood there for a while, his shoulders hunched and his hands in his britches pockets. Waiting for me to say something else, I supposed. There was nothing I wanted to say to him, though, and I turned my back.

"Come back over here, you naughty boy," Mr Farrar called across the clearing. "I can see we'll have to keep our eyes on this one."

Hobbs strode off, muttering something I couldn't hear.

"Don't be like that," Kerridge said to him. "We're only trying to keep you pure and good, aren't we, Farrar?"

His sleeping sack stayed rolled up where he'd dropped it. I had no intention of touching it, however cold I got.

HOBBS:

It was ages before I slept. My legs were aching from the walking and the rifle drill of that morning, and the ache spread itself through my whole body. That kind of ache, the ache of hard work, can be a pleasant way of sending a person to sleep, but it didn't work on me this night. Sometimes I had the drowsy feeling you get before the world goes black, but it didn't make any difference. I couldn't get to sleep. Every little movement anyone made, every swish of the grass when a breeze got up, sounded loud as ordinary speech to me.

It also seemed that I could feel the Earth turning beneath my back; with me so small and the sky so big and wide and dusted with stars. I knew those stars were moving, but no matter how close I looked I could only see them hanging there as still as water in a pond. I held my little finger up to measure the distance between two of the brightest. Less than a finger apart they looked, but the truth was that they were miles and miles away from each other. I knew that. The whole world was moving and changing but I couldn't see it. It was just like the trees around me. They were changing too. They were growing and they were dying, bit by bit.

At one point Farrar went treading off to the edge of the clearing to piss in the bushes. I could just make him out, standing there and pretending to take in the air. He wouldn't've been so shifty about it if it hadn't been for the girl.

"Watch out for ferrets, Farrar," Kerridge called after him. "Once they lock their jaws, you know, there's no shaking them off."

I got tired of their mucky talk sometimes. Like when I took the girl my sleeping sack. I only did it because I thought she might be sad and wondering about her people. I waited till it got a bit gloomy before I went over to her, to save us both embarrassment. I knew what that pair might make of it. I knew they'd see something smutty in it. The way she turned on me made me wish I hadn't bothered.

It made me mad to see her behave so suspicious. After all, I'd left my father's shop and joined the commercial volunteers for her and others like her. To fight and maybe die. That was a big fear to live with. And she couldn't even find a word of thanks for me.

Of course, there'd been no fighting so far. The

nearest I'd got to it was cutting my thumb when we were training. And there'd also been a flurry of punches back at base one time...

It had all been a mistake, really. Farrar said I had one potato more than my due and he got so cranky that he took a few swings at me. I pushed him off and backed away, but I was upset and, to tell the truth, it made me shake. If I got bothered by a half-hearted scrap over a spud, what was I going to be like when I had to face a line of the Vixen's men?

I kept thinking about things like that. Especially that night, when we were supposed to be on our way to bloody battle at Black Garlock.

You don't think, Talbot had told us. Part of your mind stops working, like someone shutting a door in it. But Talbot was a regular. He'd fought before, on foreign soil. We all knew he was up to that kind of thing. He certainly didn't know what it was to find your arms and legs trembling with fear because a skinny old boy like Farrar was aiming punches at you.

Well, that sleeping sack was there, not much more than a dozen paces off, and the darker it got the colder it got. But I wouldn't go and fetch it back. I'd bloody freeze first.

Talbot wouldn't fuss over a bit of cold. He'd hold up. That's what I was thinking when I dropped off in the end.

Talbot leading us into battle. Into smoke and honour.

And me doing my best for his sake.

And keeping proud ... and not creeping over to get that sleeping sack.

MARY:

When I opened my eyes Mr Talbot was kneeling by me. He looked as if he'd been there some moments, waiting for me to wake. I sat up quickly and turned away. It was very calm and very early. There were layers of flat grey cloud across the sky and it looked like it was going to be hot.

"What's beyond these woods?" he said quietly.

"What?"

"What are we going to find when we get out of these woods?"

"Just rough ground. The Horseback Hills on one side and farmland..."

"How far?"

"Just beyond the trees, I think."

"Both sides of the track?"

"The hills to one side and farmland the other."

"Tell me when we're near the main road. We can turn off then."

"Mr Talbot?"

"What?"

"Why must we find Black Garlock?"

He looked at me as if he was making up his mind whether to answer or not.

"We're lost," he said at last. "You've no doubt guessed that. The rest of the army is heading for Black Garlock, and so are the others."

"The others?"

"The Vixen."

"There's to be a battle?"

"Well, they won't shake hands, Mary."

He walked over to the huddled form of Mr Crowe and flicked at it with the side of his boot. It moaned and rolled over.

"Get them up. We'll be moving off in ten minutes."

Hobbs came over to get his sleeping sack. He deliberately didn't look at me. He looked creased and crumpled and I felt a little sorry for being so proud. But only a little. The others stood up stiffly, stretching and trying to shake some life back into their limbs. They didn't say much; just odd mumbles at each other in quiet voices, as if they were in a church waiting for the service to start. We were all given a handful of bread to eat on the march.

"Come on, get moving," Mr Talbot said. "Marching will get the chill out of your bones."

We found our way back to the track and started walking. The sergeant kept himself between me and the others. You could never tell what he was thinking from the look on his wall of a face, but I guessed that he was worried because he lowered his voice when he spoke to me. He doesn't trust me, I thought.

"You remember your promise to me, Mary?"

"I remember."

"You do as I say and give me directions. And you give them to me, not the others."

"I remember," I said. "You don't have to keep telling me."

We walked on for a pace or two more.

"What I do won't always make sense," he said. "That doesn't matter. You keep on as if it does, and don't say anything."

"You want me to keep my mouth shut all the way to Black Garlock?" I wanted to sound defiant. All this talk about doing as I was told, as if I was a child. I wanted him to know how silly I thought it all was. My voice failed me, though. It didn't sound defiant. It just sounded like a question.

"You can talk about anything for all I care. Except where we're going and what I'm doing."

The track beyond the woods was not much more than plain ground flattened by carts and feet over the years. It cut through a tussocky moor. There were hedges and cultivated fields a little way to the right, and here and there you could make out the silvery windings of a river, flowing down to Black Garlock itself. On our left rose the Horseback Hills. They looked like their name: a clump of rounded necks and rumps. The closest slopes were quite gentle, just hillocks really, but over in the distance the hills became much higher and more rounded.

We made our way across this open stretch for a good long time before Mr Talbot called a halt.

"Are we close to the road, Mary?" he asked.

"Not far, I think."

"It'll do, then," he said and turned round to the men. "We leave the track here," he said.

"Why?" asked Farrar. "What's special about here?"

"Nothing's special about here, Farrar. It's the road just ahead that's special. It's broad and flat, according to our map, and it makes good, soft walking."

"Then why—"

"But not for us. We're keeping off the road. There's no guarantee who you're going to run into on a highway like that. If it's the wrong lot they see you coming for miles and you don't have a chance in hell. So, we're going the hard way. All right?"

None of them said anything to that. He looked at them all and waited but no one had any more questions. Then he snatched hold of my hand. The haste in the movement shocked me.

"No," I said and tried to pull back.

"Yes, Mary. You lead the way with me."

His palm was like saddle leather, his fingers dry as stones. He stepped off the track and tugged me after him.

To the left, towards the hills.

"But this isn't..."

He tightened his grip and darted me a look full of warning. Say nothing.

And he led us onto the first slopes of the Horseback Hills. In the wrong direction.

CHAPTER
FIVE

HOBBS:
My father used to say you had to watch the women customers. Not all of them. Just the flighty pieces. They were the ones who were looking to wheedle something out of you. A bit knocked off the price of an item, or a few days extra to pay. They smile, he said, and blink their eyes and the next thing you know you've been diddled out of both time and money.

I couldn't always see this myself, though perhaps that was because it worked better on me than it did on him. Now I come to think on it, it never worked on him at all. I can't recall him knocking anything off the price for anyone; not even me when I needed a stub of candle for my room. What I do remember is backing into a stack of buckets when the girl from the bookseller's came in for some string. I'd skipped and danced round those bloody buckets, smooth as a skater, every day of every week without a moment's trouble. As soon as that girl put her head in the shop, though, and smiled, I took two great steps backwards, and down they went.

What I didn't understand was why. I mean, why did her coming in have that result? The old man said they were all out to cheat the business, but all she wanted was string.

Another time I saw her cross the street to come into the shop and I placed myself as far from damage as I could and held on to the counter to prevent myself lurching off and bundling into the mops or something. In she came, smiled and said it was a nice day and did we have any brown paper?

"Yes," I said, counting out the words as careful as I could. "It's a warm year for the time of day but we don't have any brown paper, I'm afraid."

Of course, we did have brown paper. It was on the shelf behind my head and she could probably see it. I haven't the slightest idea why I said what I did.

It was not so much the money worries that made me tread so careful with the flighty customers. It was more the way this girl had me flinging myself about like Mr Punch and talking a lot of rubbish. So my father's words of wisdom hit home.

Anyway, the point is, putting one thing with another, I began to have my doubts about this Mary who was supposed to be leading us back to our army. Not because she'd thrown my offer of the sleeping sack back in my teeth. Well, not just because of that. I began to notice other things, too. The way she'd hardly speak to us. The way she seemed so full of suspicion. Also, the way that Talbot kept his eye on her all the time. He wouldn't have done that if he didn't have his doubts, too.

I puzzled about all this as we marched, and when we came to the point on the track where we turned off, I made up my mind: she wasn't all she claimed to be. It happened like this...

Sergeant Talbot told us we were to traipse over the rough ground because main routes might be dangerous. I wouldn't've thought of that but I'm glad he did. I could just see us whistling round a bend into a pack of the Vixen's men coming the other way. Anyway, that was what he said and that was what we were going to do, and he grabbed hold of the girl and set off towards these humpy hills.

Now, this was the thing. She tried to pull away and started to say something. Then she stopped herself. Why did she do that? I thought. It took no more than a second or two, but it was there plain enough. First the pull away, then those few words of protest cut off before she said too much.

I'd no idea what was in her mind, but I didn't think it was much to do with us getting to Black Garlock. I'd've spoken out then and there, but Talbot was so quick onto it that I decided to hold my tongue. I was right glad that he was the sort of man he was and that we – dodderers and kids he called us – could be secure in our trust of him. She might be able to trick her way round us, but she wasn't up to fooling Talbot.

It was much harder going when we left the track and made for the hills. The ground was soft and full of dips and slopes. It was like walking on bed-clothes. That might be all right for five minutes but after half an hour the tops of your legs and your calves got tired.

Things weren't made any easier by the zigzag route we had to take. Most of the ground was dry and spongy, but the further we went and the higher we got the more we encountered waist-high bushes and clumps of small, thorny trees. We stopped many times. Whenever we came to a good-sized clump we took a short breather in the shade. It amazed me how the sun had shot to the top of the sky. One moment it seemed it was creeping up on our right, not particularly hot, and the next it was frying the top of your head and making the sweat dribble down your back.

It must've been early afternoon before we found a few small trees comfortable enough to rest the lot of us properly, and by then we were all ready for it. And even more ready for a bit of bread and a mouthful of warm water. I sat for a while and looked around. A strange landscape it was. The woods where we'd spent the night were no more than a green-grey blur far below us. It seemed odd to me that when we were walking through woods we stopped in a clearing, and now that we were walking plain, rough hills we stopped in a patch where there were trees. I suppose it made sense really. It just struck me as odd.

There was very little to see. Just the same rolling land everywhere. You'd have to be a rabbit or something to know your way around a place like that. Rabbits could maybe tell one hummock from the next. I couldn't, and I doubted the girl could either.

When we set off again, I had a bit more spring in my step. I went running out of our little resting place, my feet tumbled over each other down the slope, and I sent myself sprawling. I pitched straight over and the ground came up and walloped me in the face.

There was a tingling in my head that took my sight away for a moment or two. Then I hauled myself up onto my knees and the sounds of the others laughing came to my ears. Next thing I knew there was warm blood trickling down my nose and into my mouth. The worst thing about it, though, was not the pain but the picture I presented. Springing off like a fresh lamb and then nose-diving to the turf. I knew I must've looked a proper pudger.

When I tried to stand up I discovered I was still dizzy and plomped straight down again. Even more of a pudger. One by one the other lads walked by me. Not much sympathy there. Just sniggering and comments.

"It's dead easy, Hobbs," Kerridge said. "You just put one foot in front of the other. It's called walking."

"Get your bearings, lad," said Talbot without so much as a glance. "And don't fall too far behind."

Then the girl came up and stopped. Her shadow fell over me. Smiling proudly, I imagined. *What gangling idiot is this?* But she stooped down and handed me a bit of cloth.

"I'm all right," I said.

"No, you're not. Take it."

I was still dizzy enough to take it without argument. I stuffed it under my snout to stop the flow.

"Have you got any water in your pack?" she asked.

"A drop or two."

"Damp the cloth, then. It'll help."

I did as I was told and struggled to my feet. She'd already hurried off to catch up with the others. I followed with the wet cloth clamped to my face.

I thought, I'll have to thank her. Whatever she's up to. Then I remembered the sleeping sack and how she hadn't said thank you for that. Well, it seemed to me that she'd got one up on me then. I'd offered help and she'd said no. She'd offered help and I'd taken it.

Like my old man said, they have their flighty ways. You don't know what they're up to till it's all over.

MARY:

At first I thought he'd made a mistake and that's all there was to it. People muddle left and right,

57

east and west sometimes. Maybe that's what he'd done. And we didn't cut straight off the track. We went at an angle so we were still heading more or less east. If we'd borne round to the right we'd still be on course for Black Garlock. But then we began to work further into the hills, twisting and turning and climbing, going a little more left each time. So it was no mistake. He meant to go that way.

In any case, he'd been so definite about it, and so sharp with his looks. I could've just told him he was going wrong, but he was determined that I should say nothing.

There was plenty of time to think about this. We journeyed on, hour after hour, mostly in silence, well beyond the places I recognized. I guessed that somewhere ahead of us and to the right was Motley, where I thought the Campions had probably gone.

I kept wondering if they'd made it, and hoped they'd be wondering about me. It was a way of joining my thoughts with theirs. Mr Talbot said the main roads might be dangerous, though, and the Campions were travelling by cart. You could only take the cart by main roads. Then again, Mr Talbot had lied about where we were going so perhaps he'd also lied about the roads. That's the way my mind kept running. Back to the same old questions, over and over.

Eventually we came to a green mound, the topmost point of the Horseback Hills, and the sergeant called a halt. It was a relief, not just to rest but also to get ourselves above all that dry, unfriendly gorse.

"Safe enough to build a fire this time," Mr Talbot said. "We can see a good long way up here. Crowe and Webster, see if you can find some wood. Thick stuff that'll last the night. And don't for God's sake get lost."

Back down the hill they went and soon you could see no more of them than heads and shoulders, as if they were walking about in water. Hobbs ambled over to Mr Talbot with a half-purposeful look on his face, brewing up something to ask.

"How near are we now, Sergeant?" he said at last.

He had black rims of dry blood round his nostrils from his fall, and his eyes were round with tiredness.

"How near, lad? You'd better consult the map about that."

Hobbs looked at me but didn't ask. I think he was trying to frame the words in his mind, though it was a simple enough question.

"I don't know," I said before he could open his mouth.

"Come on, girl," said Mr Talbot. "You're our guide. You must have some notion."

I knew he was saying that to test me. I waited a bit and then said, "We're a good way off yet."

"That's right. We must be. If we were close we'd see signs. And there aren't any, are there?"

I thought Hobbs looked disappointed. In that

case, I thought, you'd be a sight more disappointed if you learned the truth.

"I hope you're going to be an accurate little map, Mary," said Mr Talbot, flinging his pack down on the grass. "I hope you're not leading us a dance."

Testing me again. To see if I could abide by his rules. I didn't let him down, but the only reason was that I wanted to figure out what he was up to. Also, I suppose, I couldn't trust the others. As I said, I was full of questions but there wasn't a soul I could ask. I felt even more alone out here than I had at the farm before the soldiers came.

The flaky stems of gorse that Mr Crowe and Webster brought back flared up too easily. The fire crackled a lot and was so lively that, after a short while, they had to go in search of trees that would provide heavier burning. Mr Farrar busied himself with a tin to boil up water.

"If we don't get there soon," he said, "we'll need to find a stream, or pray for rain."

The men sat round, a two and a three, looking into the flames. Hobbs and Mr Crowe. Webster, Kerridge and Mr Farrar. None of them ever sat with Mr Talbot. He was their leader, and more than a bit apart. That made it simple for me to place myself near enough to him to talk without being heard by the others.

"I want to ask something," I said.

"Go on, then."

"When we turned off the track…"

"What?"

"I said to turn right and you—"

"Turn right? Did you?"

He, too, was looking at the fire and the way the light flared and swung made the shadows move across his face. I couldn't see whether he smiled or not. His voice, soft as it was, seemed to be mocking me, but his face was just shifting shadows.

"We're going the wrong way," I said.

"Are we?"

"I've done what you said. I've kept it all to myself. But I don't really know where we are any more."

"Don't worry about that. It doesn't matter."

"But I thought I was here to show you the way."

"You are, Mary."

That use of my name. It always sounded as if it amused him.

"I can't give you any more directions," I said.

"Why not? They don't have to mean anything."

"I don't understand."

"That doesn't matter either. Just give me directions, any directions, and do what I tell you."

He turned his face to me a little and for a second or two the flames lit it fully. There was no mockery in it. Flat and unsmiling he looked. No mockery, and nothing much else either.

"You don't want to get to Black Garlock, then."

"We've a lot of walking ahead of us," he said after a pause. "You'd best get to sleep."

I'll do that when I'm ready, I thought, and I

helped myself to more tea. One of the men was snoring and I think they were all asleep. The slopes of the Horsebacks were dull and drowsy below us. Only Mr Talbot and I stayed alert. He was looking steadily into the last of the flames as if he intended to watch all night.

They treat me like a spy, I told myself. From the start that's how it's been. And all I was doing was taking food from a kitchen that was more mine than theirs.

If anyone's acting like a spy it's Mr Talbot.

HOBBS:

In the morning I washed my face in dew from the grass, which I thought a bright idea. I was mortified, though, to find I still had crusts of dry blood round my snout. I must've been a sight to see before that wash.

It's funny how a patch of plain ground, much the same as a hundred other patches, can take on such a friendly look after a while. Just because you light a fire there and sit around on the grass for an hour or so. You get to think of it differently. This bit's mine, you think. That bit's Jack's. You can get quite fond of it.

Anyway, I was pottering around, tidying up my space, when I was put in mind of the girl and how I'd still to thank her. I wasn't much looking forward to it but I didn't want her thinking I had no manners. She might have none but I had. That's one thing working in a shop gives you. Then again, maybe I just wanted to make her feel bad. I don't know.

I had no idea where the others had disappeared to – there was nowhere really to go – but the place was more or less deserted. I've a feeling Farrar and Crowe were off looking for water but I'm not sure. I do know that Talbot wasn't around. If he'd been there things wouldn't have gone on the way they did. He'd've seen to it that they stopped before they started.

I folded my sleeping sack. Stood up. Looked round. There was the girl, sitting by herself a little way off down the hill. She had her arms round her knees and she was looking back the way we'd come. Thinking I don't know what. About the farm, maybe.

Just as I started down the slope, Kerridge turned up and plomped himself down beside her. Oh well, I thought. Too late. I'll not say anything with him around. He'll only turn it into a jibe. So I went back to sorting my gear. I didn't get very far, because I was stopped by the drift of what they were saying. Or, rather, what Kerridge was saying. They had their backs to me, so they couldn't tell I was near.

"You've not said a word to us since we started," he said.

She didn't say a word then either, but that didn't put him off.

"We're your friends. We're looking after you. You ought to be a bit more friendly."

He waited a bit, no doubt to see if he'd talked her round. Which, of course, he hadn't.

"I know some girls who'd be grateful to a soldier for looking after them. I know some girls who'd know how to be friendly."

"I'm not one of them," she said.

"I can see that. But you could force yourself, couldn't you?"

He put his arm across her shoulders.

"Leave me alone," she said, quite firm but not too loud.

"You can kick up a row for all I care," said Kerridge. "I'll just say you were running off and I stopped you."

I didn't think this line of talk was right at all. I might've had my doubts about the girl but I could see this wasn't the way to go about things. You don't go in and maul people about because it takes your fancy.

"Kerridge," I said.

It wasn't a tremendous thing to say, I know, but it stunned me a bit that I'd said it, all the same. It sort of came out before I had the chance to think. It stunned Kerridge, too. He jumped up and turned round, flicking his hair out of his eyes. He wasn't best pleased to find one of his mates at his back, I could tell. He took a step towards me.

"What's up with you?" he said.

"Nothing," I said. "I just thought we ought to…"

"What?"

Well, that was a good question. Ought to what? I couldn't think. I just wanted him to get away from the girl, only I didn't want to come right out and say so.

"We ought to leave her alone, that's all."

"It looks to me as if you are leaving her alone, Hobbs. And I don't intend to. So what's next?"

"Just come away."

"Aren't you a holy man, then? Come away? Let's not be naughty boys?"

"Honestly, you talk like a pig's arse sometimes, Kerridge," I said.

I meant it as a joke. The idea was to laugh it off. It might've happened like that if I'd said it right. But I was getting nervous and there wasn't much of a laugh in my voice. For certain Kerridge didn't see the joke because, before I could say another word, he'd taken a swing at me. I just about saw it coming but that was all; I wasn't sharp enough to sway clear. He caught me smack on the nose. For half a second I could feel the end of it squashed sideways, folded against my cheek. Then, of course, my head was ringing and down came the blood again.

I'd've laughed then all right, if I'd been anyone else, watching. I mean, that nose hadn't been properly clean of blood for more than half an hour.

Out of the corner of my eye I saw the girl get up and come towards us, like she meant to stop the scrap. As far as I was concerned it had stopped. I had no mind to carry on – but what you want and what you get aren't often the same. Another of the old man's sayings.

Kerridge was winding himself up for another swing. I was quicker this time and gave him a shove on his chest. Because we were standing on a slope it unbalanced him. He tottered for a moment and then went over backwards.

"Don't fight. Leave it, please," said the girl, moving in front of me.

I was so keyed up by this point I nearly sloshed her one.

"It's all right," I said, snuffling up a trickle of blood. "I'm all right."

That was one of the funny things about me and that lass: we were always telling each other we were all right.

Kerridge picked himself up and came at me again. He was so mad by now that his face had gone red and his eyes were bulging wide.

If I'm honest I should admit that the sight didn't please me. He'd been in a few scraps, I knew; and he'd usually come out on top. For the past six weeks or so I'd been tiptoeing round, trying to stay the right side of him. Most of the time I'd been successful. Once or twice I'd overstepped the mark but managed to talk my way out of it. Now I'd made a friendly sort of remark about a pig's arse and he was charging up the hill with a damaging look in his eye.

He grabbed my tunic. He pulled me close and said things in my face. I can't remember what.

There was spit and bad language spraying off in all directions. If he wanted to hit me again he had to let go of my tunic. Well, he did want to, and he did let go, but I hit him first. It was as much a surprise to me as it was to him, I should imagine.

His head rocked back and lolled forward again, like it was on a spring. I jabbed him again. With my other fist this time: my first had a stabbing pain on the knuckle. He'll do you proper for this, I was thinking, so don't give him the chance. He staggered back again and crumpled over, rolling a little down the hill so that both legs went over his head.

Then Talbot came running up.

"What's going on here?" he said.

"I'm sorry, Sergeant. I've just hit Kerridge."

"What for, man?"

"He hit me, Sergeant. Sorry."

Kerridge hauled himself to his knees and fingered his lips. I glanced down at my knuckle and saw a little ear-shaped flap of skin, and more drops of blood. It must've been made by one of Kerridge's teeth. At this rate I was going to be injured out of the service before we ever reached a battle.

"Get to your feet," said Talbot with a snap. "And the both of you, come over here."

He stepped off to the patch of hill by his gear. That's what I mean about the place becoming sort of familiar. It was his space.

"I won't ask again what all that was about," he said. "You wouldn't tell me and I can guess anyway. All I'm saying is: leave the girl alone.

The pair of you. Yes?"

Kerridge looked down and mumbled something I took to be yes. I neither spoke nor moved. Talbot had got it wrong: he thought we were both making a try for the girl. I was keen to put that matter straight but now wasn't the time. It wouldn't've improved things.

"If we were back at camp I'd have you both lashed to a gun wheel for a touch of the rope's end. You wouldn't feel like any larking after that, I can promise you. As we're stuck in the middle of nowhere, and we're all going to need our strength, I'm going to pretend it didn't happen. Now apologize to each other."

We gave each other a sideways glance. It made me think of two little figures I'd seen on a clock once. I was sure I'd see revenge in Kerridge's eye, but I was wrong. He almost had his old grin back: he bore me no bad feelings.

By God, I was relieved.

CHAPTER SIX

MARY:

If anyone's acting like a spy…

I hardly meant it when I first said it to myself. But after that it all made sense. It was like being woken up with cold water. Suddenly your eyes are wide open and everything is sharp and clear.

Knowing didn't help, though. It just made me more frightened. And I couldn't bear to look at Mr Talbot. Couldn't bear the sight of his hard face. The more I thought about what it all meant, the more frightened I became. And it didn't get me anywhere. My mind just filled with terrible things I couldn't control.

We set off walking again and I started to talk to Hobbs. Not because I wanted to, particularly, but simply to stop all that thinking.

"I hope you weren't in too much trouble," I said.

"No." He looked startled that I'd spoken. "We

got off light because of the circumstances."

"Circumstances?"

"Us being on our way to a battle."

"Oh. I see. I'm glad. That he wasn't too hard on you, I mean."

"He didn't like it, mind. We'd displeased him."

We'd come down from the hill and were tramping through gorse again. Quite steeply down and more or less into the early sun: we were still heading east. Butterflies flickered above the tops of the bushes and every so often a fat fly rose out of the undergrowth and buzzed round my face. Hobbs walked on with his eyes fixed straight ahead. He didn't turn an inch to look at me. I think I was making him feel uncomfortable. I could understand that. I'd shown him no friendliness.

"I wanted to say thank you," I said.

"You did?"

"Yes. For what you did. I was grateful."

"What did I do?"

"Stepping in like that when Kerridge was—"

"Oh, that. That's all right."

"How's your nose?"

He did smile when I said that, only quietly and to himself. It was an odd-sounding remark, I suppose.

"It's all right. I've had it squashed to left and right. Twice in a day. They say things come in threes, though, don't they?"

"I hope they're wrong."

"So do I. There's not many more ways it can

70

be squashed." He was silent for a bit and then he added, "The thing is, I wanted to say thank you, too."

"To me?"

"Yes. For sorting out my first nosebleed."

"I didn't do much."

"It was kind, though. So thank you."

He made it sound very correct, as if we were having tea and I'd passed him some cake. Also as if he was pleased he'd got it over with. Well, so it was for both of us, I suppose.

"Talbot said I wasn't to talk to you again," he went on.

Of course. Mr Talbot would say that.

"You'd better stop, then," I snapped back. "If it worries you."

"No, no. He won't mind me thanking you. He's a fair man."

"Is he?"

"Yes, when you get to know him…"

"Well, I don't trust him."

"Why ever not?"

I couldn't tell him. I'd already said more than I intended.

"I … I don't know," I said. "The way he bullies people to do what he wants."

"That's just his job. That's what sergeants have to do. He's an upright man, though; a proper regular. And we have to abide by his rules because he's the sergeant. That's all there is to it."

"He's not my sergeant."

"No, but you're here for your own safety, aren't you?"

Safety? Was I? I could have said a thing or two about that. I could have shouted out that we were lost; that the good sergeant was a liar and for all we knew he was leading us to destruction.

But I didn't. Because I was obeying his orders just as much as Hobbs was.

Just the same. Abiding by his rules. Only with me it was out of confusion. Confusion and fear.

HOBBS:

We came right down to a string of full-sized trees, and that was a real relief. Especially after clump upon clump of spiky bushes sticking into you and plucking you back like they didn't want you to go on. And never going once from point to point in a direct line so that half the time you got the impression you were going back the way you'd just come.

Through the lower branches of these trees you could see a kind of silvery light, and I thought at first that they must've been on the brow of another hill and that I was looking at patches of sky. The nearer we got, though, the more the light seemed to tremble and break up. Then came the sound of flapping and thudding and that settled it. We'd come to a lake and we were hearing the beat of a swan's wings.

That was even more of a relief than the trees, I can tell you. A sweet sight, that lake was, after the heat of the downhill march. The trembling on the surface of the water where the warm breeze swept it, and the glassy areas where the breeze couldn't reach. Perhaps it was because of all the walking we'd been doing, but I did think that lake was one of the most beautiful places I'd ever seen.

It was early evening when we reached the shore and we made our third camp there. When we'd stowed our gear and found plenty of good wood for a fire, Kerridge, Farrar and Webster went for a dip. I would've gone in, too, but I had things to think about. I couldn't think while I was splashing about.

And to tell the truth, there was another reason. I couldn't swim.

I sat on the bank, watching those three in the water. Their shouts went skimming over the surface and they hunched their white shoulders in the chill. I was watching, but my mind kept drifting away to my chat with the girl.

She'd told me she didn't trust Talbot. It muddled me up, that did. If she was against us, and she really meant us harm, she wouldn't have said that, surely. She would've pretended she was all for him.

That was one thing. Another was, it surprised me that she didn't like him. He was a fine man: I knew no finer. So what did she see in Talbot that put her out? He spoke softly to her, like a gentleman. He had her interests at heart. *Why* didn't she like him?

There was only one way to find that out: I'd have to ask her. At any other time I'd've been content to leave things as they were, but this wasn't any other time. This was now and our lives might be at stake. We were heading for a battle. If I had my doubts I ought to sort them out now. So up I got and went to look for her.

I found her wandering further along the shore. A bit careless, I thought, to let her out of our sight like that. Under the circumstances. Not like Talbot to allow that to happen. As it turned out he hadn't been as casual as I thought, but I had no way of knowing that then.

We walked towards each other for a step or two. She smiled but I didn't smile back.

"I've been pondering what you said," I told her.

I was coming straight to the point. No dillying around with chat about what a lovely place this was and so on. She had to know I had serious things to say to her.

"I didn't say much," she said.

"You did about Talbot. He has to take charge, though. Can't you see that?"

"I know. It's not that that worries me."

"What does, then?"

"I told you: I don't trust him."

"I gathered that, but that's daft, that is. I know him. We all know him. You don't. And we don't know you."

We were walking side by side. More strolling than walking, really. When I said this she stopped and looked at me. I thought about the girl from the bookseller's but cleared the thought out of my head. There must be no ploughing into buckets now. I'd got to get this right.

"You mean I'm the one who shouldn't be trusted?" she said.

"Well, there's a few odd things I've noticed, I must say."

"About me?"

"You show us the way but you don't look like you're pleased to do it."

"Why should I be?"

"Well, we're here to fight the Vixen. Aren't you pleased about that?"

She said nothing so I plunged on.

"And yesterday, when we set out over the hills. You didn't look right about that either."

"No."

"No?"

"Look, I can only say I mean no ill. I can't prove it. If you don't believe me, that's too bad."

"But we have to be able to trust what you're doing. You're supposed to be our map."

"You still think I'm a spy, don't you?"

"I'm not saying that."

"You've talked to Mr Crowe about this, haven't you?"

"No, I haven't."

I don't know why I hadn't. It would've been a good idea because Crowe had a real knack for working things out. Too late for that now, though.

"I don't want to go behind your back," I said. "If I have my doubts it's only fair to put them to you straight."

"But what can I say? If you have your doubts

you won't believe me anyway."

"Is there nothing you can tell me, then, to put my mind at rest? Because I'd like to believe you."

And I would've liked to. If she could only have said something to settle my worries, I'd've been content. It would've been so much better to trust her.

"Perhaps I can," she said.

She paused. She was thinking hard. But I don't know what she planned to say because she never got the chance: Talbot appeared. One moment I was looking at her, the next I was looking at him. He'd popped from behind a tree or something. He must've been around for some time.

"I thought you'd understood me, lad," he said to me.

"Yes, Sergeant. I did."

"Then this is not good. I told you not to speak to Mary. And yet here you are doing just that."

"I know, but..."

"I can't be doing with that. If I give an order I must know it will be obeyed."

"He wasn't bothering me," said the girl.

"That's not the point."

For a moment we didn't speak. My mind was racing. I thought I could tell him the purpose of my chat, but I hesitated. It wouldn't have been fair of me. The girl said there was no harm in her and I was coming round to believe her. I had no evidence for it but I didn't think she was lying. I couldn't tell Talbot that now. It would've brought trouble to her and if there was trouble to be had it must be mine.

"You get back to the camp," he said to her. "I'll talk to you later."

"He's done no harm. He only—"

"I know what he's done. You take yourself off. I have to sort things out with this soldier."

So that was that. There was trouble ahead all right. And it was most certainly mine.

MARY:
He had to stand to attention with full pack on his back and rifle at the ready. Not eating or drinking. Saying nothing. Looking straight ahead and nowhere else. Motionless, with no purpose, like something on a mantelpiece.

And this was because he'd exchanged a few words with me. Not because he'd tried to be too friendly, as Kerridge had. I'm certain the sergeant knew it wasn't that.

It went on for hours, it seemed to me. Darkness fell and still he stood there, outside the ring of firelight. You'd've thought he was a tree but for a very slight wavering, side to side, now and again and occasionally the blink of his eyes.

His mates never glanced in his direction. Not once. To them he was like a ghost. Don't look and there'll be nothing there. Nothing to worry about. No mention was made of him either.

"Why don't you give him something to eat?" I said to Webster when I could bear it no longer.

77

"I can't," said Webster. "Not allowed."

He sat with the soles of his feet touching, the way a child does. When he answered me he looked down at his fingers and wiggled them slowly up and down. He was a decent lad, but slow thinking.

"It wouldn't help, miss," said Mr Crowe. "There'd be more trouble for him, and punishment for whoever helped him."

"Then I'll take him something…"

"Please don't, miss. He'll be there longer if you do."

"But don't you care? Why won't any of you look at him?"

I glanced over at Mr Talbot, who was stretched out a little way off with his hands folded beneath his head.

"It's him," I said. "He has no heart."

"It's not him," said Mr Farrar. "It's the army. Regulations."

Kerridge swallowed some tea and looked up at me. The first time he'd looked me in the eye since the fight. He stretched his neck and lifted his thin face. That movement, and perhaps the firelight, made him look unusually grave.

"I'm right sorry, too, girl," he said. "There's nothing wrong with Hobbs. But he got off light. That's the truth of it. He could've had a whipping for disobeying orders."

And there we were back to orders again. They couldn't think for themselves. Someone else had to do it for them. If it was someone like Mr

Talbot, so much the worse.

I got up and walked away from the fire, down to the lake. The water was still and black and the trees on the other shore as dark and solid as a mountain. I'd heard of this lake – Mr Campion once rode over to fish it – but I'd forgotten its name. There was a kind of map in my head. The farm was away on the left; Black Garlock was down somewhere on the right. This lake was up at the top. An indistinct shape on the very edge of what I knew. I had no idea what was beyond it.

I heard footsteps behind me, stepping from the grass to the gravelly shore, and turned to see a murky figure framed by the orange glow of the camp-fire. I knew it was Mr Talbot. And why he'd come. He'd settled Hobbs. Now it was my turn. Not for punishment, perhaps, but for one of his reminders about the rules.

"Why are you doing this?" I asked before he could speak.

"Hobbs, you mean? He disobeyed an order, like Farrar said."

"Oh yes, of course. To stop him bothering me."

"He knows why he's standing there."

"He's standing there because you're afraid of what I'll say to him, not what he might say to me. I doubt he knows that."

"You're becoming bold and familiar, Mary," he said after a silence.

"What would you have done if I'd told him what I know?" I said, turning away from him to stare out over the water.

"And what do you know?"

"That you're keeping the truth from them."

"You wouldn't have told him. I was close enough to the pair of you to step in at any moment."

"You are, though, aren't you? Keeping things from them?"

"They're not ready to know the truth, Mary."

He moved beside me.

"We're not going to Black Garlock," he said. "I'll admit that much."

"You plan to hand them over, don't you? Them and me?"

"Hand them over?"

"Yes. To the Vixen's men."

"Is that what you think?" he asked and there was a note of surprise in his voice I'd not heard before. Everything else he'd said had been so steady and knowing.

"If that's what you plan," I told him softly, "you'll have to kill me, Sergeant."

But I won't make it easy for you, I thought. I guessed at the distance between us. More than an arm's length. If he wanted to silence me now I could run. He might catch me in the end, and he might talk those foolish men round to his way, but I'd make it as hard as I could for him. I'd kick and shout out.

He made no move, though. He didn't even look my way but kept a level gaze at the lake. When he

80

spoke his voice was level, too. Low and intense.

"I don't want to kill you. I don't want anyone to die. You look at them, Mary, and tell me what you see. A group of soldiers, is it? Fighting men? Do you see Webster? He's a baker, did you know that? A simple lad who never had a harmful thought in his life. Put him in a soldier's tunic and he's still a baker. And bad-tempered Farrar. Life's not treated him well: he's disappointed in it. But that's no reason why he should give it up. And Kerridge. Kerridge is no more than a kid. He's not stupid though he acts it sometimes. He likes to enjoy himself. Well, why not? Then there's Jack Crowe. Can you see Jack in the firelight? Has he got his nose in a book? He has more ideas in that bald noddle of his than I'll ever have in mine. And he'd throw all that away to defend his native soil. Very noble of him, but he doesn't know what it means to do that. Not really. His ideas don't stretch that far.

"Are you understanding me now, Mary? Do you see what I've got on my hands?

"What about young Hobbs, then? There he stands, stiff and obedient. Like a tin soldier in a kiddy's box. I like Hobbs. Maybe you don't believe me, but I do. I like the way he tries his best and gets it wrong. I like the way he whistles and doesn't know he's doing it."

He stopped talking for a while and I heard him sigh.

"Yes, it's army regulations that make him stand

to attention half the night. I use army regulations. But I'm supposed to take that crew to Black Garlock and watch them march into battle against the Vixen. Watch them drop and die. It might be different if they were proper soldiers but they're not. And I don't see the sense in it. Do you?"

I didn't answer for a long while. I couldn't. He turned away from the lake and there was just enough light for me to make out his face. That same blank wall, as if there were no feelings behind it.

"What about you?" I said.

"Me? Well, I am a soldier. That's my job. Do you know what they say about us? A soldier in peace time is like a chimney in summer. Not a bit of use. That bothered me at one time. Not any more."

"You mean you're leading them away from battle?"

"Yes."

"Where?"

"I don't know and it doesn't much matter. We have no destination, Mary. We're just going away."

CHAPTER SEVEN

Hobbs:
The darker it got, the better I felt.

To begin with, they were all sitting round the fire and I was at attention a yard or two away and it looked like I was the last skittle standing. They were decent about it, mind. There was no taunting. And I'd been expecting worse. You can never see much in Talbot's eyes but when he found me talking to the girl I was convinced I was in for a flogging at least. When all I had to do was stand guard in full kit, I thought I had two birthdays in the month. And that's the way I continued to feel.

For the first half hour.

Beyond that, the sweat started to dribble down the sides of my head, my neck and back, and my brain started to go off on its own. I say half an hour but I've no idea, really. An hour, two hours. Once you lose track you can never get back.

In the end I felt like a perfect round ball of

darkness in the middle of a bigger darkness and hardly any different from it. Then a voice came at me from somewhere. It might've been the voice of God. It said words I couldn't fathom. It said them over and over.

"All right, Hobbs. That'll do. That's enough."

Then pressing somewhere. My elbow. And for a spell that was the centre of me. That was Hobbs. A living elbow.

But bit by bit I came out of the darkness and heard Talbot's voice, and felt him lead me into the firelight. He helped me down onto the ground and spread out my sleeping sack. I think I'd started to tremble.

The girl came and gave me something to drink. I saw her pale face. I said things without considering the words.

"Not flighty," I said. "You're not flighty. The old man got it wrong. I like you, Mary. I like you and there's no harm in that, is there?"

And rambling on, the same things all jumbled up. I know I said this because much later she laughed and told me about it. If I'd not had to stand out there in the dark, I'd never have said such things. It just shows you: good comes from bad sometimes.

I'd made up my mind about her while my thoughts were off somewhere the other side of the stars.

MARY:
We didn't set off straight away in the morning as we

84

had done at our other camps. By now we were getting short of food so the men went off to see what they could find.

"Three rounds," Mr Talbot told them. "But only if it's necessary. Take Farrar's rifle. He's the only one with a chance of hitting anything."

They all looked different in the morning light. Especially the sergeant. I suppose I don't mean that. He looked just the same but I saw him differently. It was no simple matter to hate him after that. I did try for a while but hating him didn't fit.

And the others. I'd always thought of them as the others. Or the men. Now, as I watched them off on their hunting expedition, I found myself thinking of them by their names. Mr Farrar, who was sad about life. Mr Crowe, who read books and was prepared to die for his country. They weren't just a group with one dull mind. They had their different ways of doing things, and their different thoughts. And they were all here by chance, just as I was.

They disappeared into a thick grove which ran down to the water's edge. I heard the swish and crackle of the undergrowth. Hobbs whistling. Mr Crowe telling them all to be quiet in a small, fading voice.

"They'll come back with something," Mr Talbot said at my back. "We'll build up the fire in preparation, you and me."

We set about this and for a long spell nothing was said by either of us. There was a lot I wanted to say – and ask – but I didn't know how to begin.

"You're quiet this morning, Mary," he said eventually.

"We both are."

"You've thought about what I said last night?"

"Of course I have."

"And does it make a difference?"

"I suppose so."

"What kind of difference?"

"I'm not sure, but you must tell them at some point. We can't just go on and on walking into the country and getting nowhere."

"I know. But if I tell them now they'll turn round and head back. Jack Crowe would see to that. I'll tell them when we're far enough off."

"You won't let them decide for themselves?"

"No. I can't do that."

He tipped a huge log onto the fire and a flurry of sparks rose into the air. We sat down with the flames between us and waited for it to catch.

"This is your country, too," I said. "And it's been invaded. Don't you want to do all you can to save it?"

"Invaded?" he said. "Who by, do you know?"

"Of course I know. The Vixen."

"The Vixen!" He huffed through his nose and began to pick at his boots with a twig.

"And she's come to take our home. Our land that belongs to us."

"So they tell us."

"Don't you care, then?"

"I care about what I can understand, Mary."

"And what's that?"

"That it's better to live than die."

"That's what cowards say."

"Oh? I'm a coward, am I?"

"You're running away. You're afraid to admit that to your men. Yes. You're a coward."

I held my breath and looked at him through the flames. I said what I did to sting him, and then waited for him to hit back. I saw the yellow tongues waving and flickering. I saw his hunched shape beyond them.

"You don't know what you're saying," he said, still poking the twig at his boots.

"I do. And I depend on soldiers to protect me. You're afraid to do that."

"You've not seen a battle. Nor have they. It's not that easy." His voice dropped so low that I could hardly tell it from the spluttering of the fire. "I'll tell you what it's like, though it'll only be words. You'd have to be there to know."

"We had a campaign near the beginning of last year," he began. "Overseas. Why we were there doesn't matter.

"There was a strip of farmland between two forests. A narrow field for a battle but that's where it was to be. I was to be sergeant at the colours. That means I had to march by our banner. Not holding it – we had a young kid for that – but keeping an eye on it should it fall. There's always the chance of that because the fighting is thickest round the banners. If you see your banner go down, the heart can go out of you. If they lose theirs your heart gets hotter for the fight.

"It's both an honour and a curse to be sergeant at the colours. It's an honour because you know your mates will look to you and you fight directly under the symbol of all you care about. You know what that means, Mary: king and country. But it's a curse because more men will die at the banners than will live.

"We formed a square and advanced. Steady, steady advance. All together. Under control. Up ahead the enemy line. Their gunners standing tall and wide awake. A troop of horse. All waiting. But you're inside the marching square and you feel safe, shoulder to shoulder with mates.

"That's like a lot of things in a battle: it's false. You're not safe there at all.

"First came the fire of their heavy guns. Deep, rocking explosions as they were gauging their distances. The shots that fell closest caused smoke to drift across the front ranks. And smoke is another false thing in battle. Nothing looks right in smoke, especially when things start to burn and flare. You see figures nearly twice their natural size. And you can't tell friend from foe. I've known men kill their closest mates in smoke.

"That's the way it began. According to the books. But you can't say how it went on. All you know is what happens within a short stone's throw of where you stand. And you can't always remember what happens then. A man dies on your right. A man dies at your back. Which died first? You can't remember. If you live, and can talk about it afterwards, you might piece things together. You might not. All you know for sure is that certain things happen in flashes, like shells going off.

"I'll tell you some of the things that happened that day.

"A ball came through the second rank a yard or two to my right. I saw it take a man's arm off at the shoulder. I saw it pass through a country boy called Seth. Christ, I've prayed that more men could die as quick and clean as that in the battles I've fought. That they aren't left screaming on the ground as their mates go treading on over them.

"At some point there were bodies piled up in front of me. Piled up. High as my shoulder. And some were dead and some were not because I saw them move.

"A shell landed at the feet of that boy with the banner. I threw myself down, but the boy just stood there. He looked at it as if he was curious to see what it was. The blast blew his hand away. I snatched up the banner and there was the boy, still standing there. He smiled at me. Held out his hand to take the banner back. But he had no hand left. He lifted his arm and his blood struck my tunic. And still he smiled. I bound up the arm as best I could and he carried on with the banner clamped to his side with his good hand.

"They told us we took the day. The battle was ours. Some men cheered to hear that news. We all stretched out on the ground to sleep. Just where we stood. There were men still injured, good mates, crying out for help. We found a space to sleep and left them where they were. That's what you did. Dropped in your tracks. You could do no other.

"Hours later we began to carry the wounded back. We took those who looked as if they had a chance. The others we left.

"I'd lost track of the boy who'd carried the banner. But next day, back at camp, there he was by one of the surgeon's tents, upright, talking, laughing. Instead of a hand a bloody stump wrapped in dirty white cloth. I was pleased to see him and thanked God for saving the lad.

"Then I went up to ask him how he was doing. He talked and talked. About the battle, the things he'd seen, the things he'd done as a kiddie. Talk, talk. Anything that flew into his head. He barely stopped talking for two more days. Then he fell silent entirely. The shell had taken his hand and wiped his mind clean as a schoolboy's slate.

"He was seventeen, just turned. About the same as Hobbs, I reckon. They sent him home with a pension that was just enough to pay for the chair he sits in now, all day. He sits there staring down, same as when that shell landed. His mother looks after him like she did when he was small.

"I know this to be true because she's my

wife and Jamie is our boy."

What could I say after I'd heard his story? I searched for things that might be a comfort to him but it wouldn't have been right to say them. The correct thing to do was to sit still and think on what he'd said.

He was a man with a wife and a son the same age, more or less, as Hobbs and Kerridge. And they'd gone off hunting, fit and running and sound in their minds.

Mr Talbot stood up and started stripping the bark off a long green stick to make a spit for the fire. He whittled away at it for a while and then said:

"This is not an order, Mary, but no one knows what I've just told you, saving my commanding officer and some of the other sergeants from that campaign... What I'm asking is that you keep it to yourself."

"Of course I shall," I said.

"Thank you. I only told you because I wanted you to understand why I'm doing this."

"I know."

"And do you understand?"

"Yes," I said. I swallowed and held my breath for a moment before going on. "But I still think you should explain it to the men."

"That I can't do."

"They're all old enough. They can make up their own minds."

"I'll tell them when the time is right," he said. "You let me be the judge of that."

HOBBS:

We came back loaded with game. Some ducks and a swan – poor, pretty thing. It near broke my heart to see its lovely neck swinging down at Kerridge's back so loose and lifeless. But these things have to be done. I know that.

The sergeant and Mary were still circling each other like dogs weighing up the chances of a fight. I had the feeling they'd spent the whole time we were away in a moody silence. I thought that was a shame because I was sure a bit of chat between them would've sorted out their differences. However, they'd built a good fire between them and we wasted no time in roasting the birds over it. The fat hissed into the flames and the smell came off so rich and savoury it almost laid me out.

We only had a taste of the meat, though. Most of it was for wrapping up and carrying with us. Talbot was standing there at the fire, with his arms folded, watching Webster turning the spit. He reckoned there'd be enough to see us to the end of our journey; to see us all the way to Black Garlock.

"Can I ask a favour, Sarge?" I said to him in a voice the others weren't meant to hear. I was standing next to him, I noticed, so I thought I'd take my chance.

"A favour, Hobbs?" he said.

"I mean permission, Sergeant."

"What for?"

"Well, I've had my punishment and learned my lesson. At least, I hope I have. But…"

"Well, what is it?"

He wasn't lowering his voice in the way I was. I leaned a little bit closer so he should see I meant this to be private.

"I'd like permission to speak to Mary again. There's … well, there's things I might have to say."

"Oh, are there?" he boomed out.

My face was burning. Maybe he thought it was from being so close to the fire. I hoped so.

"I think so," I said. "You see, I don't know that I was in my right mind before I went to sleep last night. I've a feeling I … said things."

"What sort of things, Hobbs?"

"I'm not sure. Things I might have to apologize for."

"Oh. I see. Well, well, well."

He nodded his head and pondered, and nodded his head a bit more. It took him ages. I'm not sure, but I think he was doing it on purpose. I was nodding my head with him in the end. I couldn't help it: it was catching.

"So," I said after about a month of this, "can I have permission to speak?"

"I think you'd better, lad. I think you ought to put that record straight. We mustn't offend our map, must we?"

It wouldn't have surprised me to see the whole lot of them gathered round after that performance, waiting to see what I planned to do next. I'd only meant it to be a word on the quiet. Luckily, though, they had their eyes fixed on the roasting birds and hadn't noticed a thing. So I shuffled round till I was next to Mary.

"I'd like a chat," I said. "If that's all right."

She nodded quickly, thank heavens, and we moved away, walking down to the lake. We took our time, just ambling, and I kept looking back at the others to see that they were occupied.

"Look," I explained. "I've had a word with Sergeant Talbot and he says it's all right…"

"What is?" she asked.

"For me to speak to you."

"Oh? You asked him, did you?"

Good Lord, Hobbs, I said to myself, why did you start all this? It was getting harder to make myself understood by the minute.

"Look, I only want to say one thing. I just don't want to end up standing to attention in the middle of a field for saying it, that's all."

"What is it, then?"

"Right." I took a breath. "I'm sorry."

"What?"

"I wanted to say sorry…"

"Oh, Hobbs," she said, and I do believe she smiled to herself which made me squirm more. "Not again."

"What do you mean, not again?"

"You're always saying sorry, or thank you. I've never met a lad so polite."

"It's the way I was brought up," I said, but I made that sound like I was saying sorry, too.

"Well, I don't understand. What are you sorry for this time?"

"It's a bit hard to explain. Only, I think I might've said a thing or two last night that was a bit ... a bit..."

"What?"

"That's just it. I'm not sure but I might've been rude."

"You weren't rude, Hobbs."

"What did I say, though?"

"Well..."

"What?"

"You said I wasn't flighty."

"Oh, no."

"That's all right, though. It isn't rude, is it?"

"Was that all?"

Then she laughed and I feared the worst. I must've said something daft if it made her laugh.

"You said you liked me, and that there was nothing wrong in that."

"Oh, no."

"No? You didn't mean it?"

"No. I mean, yes. Yes, it's true. But I shouldn't have said it."

"Then I forgive you for speaking your mind. If that's what you were doing."

We'd stopped walking and were facing each other. She wasn't a tall lass. The top of her head only came up to my shoulder. I was still wriggling inside, like a worm on a hook, but I was partly glad I'd told her I liked her.

"You've said more than your one thing by now," she said with a smile.

"I suppose I have."

"Then you ought to stop by rights."

"I ought to've stopped long ago," I said.

MARY:

When we'd shared out some of the meat, and packed up the rest, we got ready to leave. Mr Talbot made a fuss about which way we should go. Left or right round the lake. No one would move till I'd had my say. They all stood there gaping at me, like they'd done on the track when I really did know the way. It saddened me to see their faces so full of trust and hope. I said left. It didn't make any difference.

The way was clear and easy which was a piece of good luck. It might've been a lovely walk, too, with the lake on one side and woods on the other, but I hardly paid it much attention. The men were weighed down by their packs, as they always had been, and I was labouring under a different kind of burden. It was knowing what I did – about the sergeant's son and about his plan – that made the going so hard. I thought better of him now, but he was making me act a lie and that I didn't like. I'd lied to him back at the farm and it was a thing that didn't come easy to me. Here I was, leading them I knew not where, and every step I took was false.

A new kind of lie.

There was nothing I could do about it, however. It was bad to be fooling them like that but it would've been worse to break Mr Talbot's trust. If I'd betrayed that I would've piled more hurt on his head.

I could hear Hobbs lumbering along behind me. He wasn't the most fluent mover. I pushed a branch out of my path and heard it swish back and catch him a swipe.

"Sorry," I said. "Are you all right?"

"Oh, yes. It didn't hurt."

"You've never told me what your name is. Your first name, I mean."

"No."

"Is it a secret?"

"No, I suppose not."

But he didn't go on.

"The sergeant's well behind us," I said. "He won't know you're talking."

"I suppose he won't."

"Shall I ask permission first? Would that make you happier?"

"It's Arthur," he said, almost as if he was ashamed of it. "But I think I prefer Hobbs."

"Arthur?"

"Yes. Keep your voice down."

"Where's your home, Arthur?"

"I live with my father above our shop. We're all from shops, we are. Commercial volunteers. Webster's a baker. Crowe comes from a bank…"

"Isn't that strange? That you should all be shop people turned to soldiers?"

"No. It's not strange. When we got word of the invasion we all joined up together. There's a whole regiment of shop lads. And another of factory men."

"Some of the men from the farm went off to join up, too. Maybe they have a regiment of farmhands."

"I should think they have," he said. "You won't tell the others, will you?"

"What?"

"About my name. Only they don't know and…"

"Not more secrets."

"More? What else is there, then?"

"It doesn't matter."

I was talking to keep my mind busy but it didn't really work. There was something about this conversation, me in front and his voice with no face to it, that put me in a taunting mood. Poor Hobbs. He couldn't have known why.

"What do you sell in your shop, Arthur?"

"Mops and buckets. Pots and pans. Nothing of interest."

"No?"

"It interests Dad, but not me. He likes to make profit. He'd sell me if I stood still long enough."

"Will you go back to it, then, Arthur? If all this ends?"

"I don't know. Mary."

"I don't care if you call me Mary. It's my name."

He didn't say anything to that. I took a quick look over my shoulder to see if he was still there. He was treading along with his eyes to the ground, looking downcast and thoughtful.

"When we get to the battle," he said slowly, almost stopping to think after each word, "it'll all be a muddle, I've no doubt. There'll be all manner of comings and goings..."

"Are you sure there'll be a battle?"

"There must be. Everyone says so. But I can't think what it'll be like. It frightens me, the thought of it. A soldier shouldn't be frightened but I don't reckon myself a proper soldier. I hope you don't mind me going on like this?"

"No."

"I want to tell someone. The thing is, though, I'd like to write you a letter."

"A letter?"

"Yes. Would you let me do that?"

"I'd like a letter from you."

"I think I'll feel more content about things if I can do that. You won't have to read it."

"Of course I'll read it. I promise. But you must sign it Arthur for me."

He laughed out loud, so suddenly that it made me jump. I was glad that we couldn't see each other, that he didn't know I was trying not to weep. For Arthur Hobbs, preparing himself to face a battle. For what I knew but he didn't. For the letter he wanted to send to a girl with no address and no home.

CHAPTER
EIGHT

HOBBS:
It was the daftest talk I ever had.

For one thing we shouldn't've been talking at all. The last time I'd spoken to Mary without asking for Talbot's say-so I'd got done for it. Regulation punishment. If he catches me this time, I thought, he'll have me swimming round that lake in full kit. I can't swim but that wouldn't stop him. Still, he was well to the back of the line, and I didn't want her to think I only did what I was told. So I persuaded myself: the sergeant's not an unreasonable man. He wouldn't object to a simple chat.

For another thing the whole conversation was carried out with her back to me. I couldn't see her face at all. This turned out to be a good thing in the end, mind. Not that I didn't want to see her. It's just that things wouldn't have taken the turn they did if I'd been looking at her all the time. I'd've been too nervous.

But the main thing was the cracked things we talked about. They'd make a cat laugh. My name. The shop. I hadn't wanted to tell her about either of those things. They were ordinary and drab. Arthur. I hate the name. A lad might as well be called Pudger. Pudger Hobbs. It's all right if you're a king, I suppose. But a shop boy ought to be called something else.

It was funny talk. But not just funny. Serious, too. Like things you say in your dreams.

I asked her about the letter.

It was the thought of battle that made me do that. Every step taking us that bit closer.

I thought, well, she can laugh at me if she likes. I'm still going to ask.

MARY:

Webster paused by a small inlet of shallow water and thin reeds. He stood there looking and the others gathered behind him to see what the matter was. A duckling was darting over the surface of the water in a panic. It went in tight circles, round and round, giving out faint peeping cries because it couldn't see its mother. After a moment or two, Kerridge unhitched his pack and waded into the water. He shushed the duckling gently out onto the lake. Mr Talbot watched all this without protest.

Eventually the duckling caught sight of its mother and swam off. Kerridge took up his pack again and we carried on walking. No one said a word about it.

I think this happened because the men thought they were getting nearer to the moment of battle; to the day that might be their last. They became two things at once. More tender. But hardened to thoughts of danger and killing. Both these things at the same time. It was strange.

I noticed how Mr Crowe would sit by himself. And how Mr Farrar had taken to reading. He did this when he thought no one was paying attention, and he hid the book in the crook of his arm. It was a battered little prayer book. I think we all knew, though no one ever mentioned it.

I could not bear all this.

They were facing up to the idea of death, yet I knew that it was all a lie.

We reached the other side of the lake, went on another mile or so as evening came down, and stopped to make our fourth camp. We were by a forest of tall, grey trees. The land ahead of us sloped up gently to the brow of a low hill. There was no telling what was beyond that. There was a strong feeling in the men that this would be our last stopping-place.

"You must tell them," I said to Mr Talbot.

"There'll be a time for that," he answered in his calm voice.

"If you don't, I shall. I've kept my promise up to now but it isn't right any more."

"They won't believe you," he said simply. "Their lives have been in my hands for too long. They trust me. Besides, they won't want to believe you."

He looked at me steadily.

"You think I'm wrong?" he said. "Then tell them and see."

But I couldn't. He knew that I couldn't. And I couldn't wait until he thought the time was right, either. Not with Mr Farrar thumbing through his old prayer book, and Jack Crowe staring into his own dark thoughts.

I didn't plan what I did next.

Mr Talbot left me and I sat with my back to a fallen tree, thinking about all that had happened. About Mr Talbot and his son. About the Campions and Lizzie. About Hobbs.

When I blinked and came out of these thoughts, I was surprised to see that the softness of evening had deepened into a warm darkness, right into the thick of night. The men were busy with this and that. Some might've been stretched out on their sacks asleep. I don't really know what they were doing. They weren't paying me any attention.

So I stood up, turned my back on them, and walked away.

HOBBS:

I picked up this piece of branch and started to chip at it with my knife. Curls of white came off, very clear in the dark, and you could smell the wood. It was twisted in a funny way that made it look like the parson's hand when he gives the blessing, and it was the colour of bone. I ran the blade round it, cutting out a double line, like a couple of cuffs.

Then I began to carve patterns – triangles and zigzags and what have you, getting more and more ornate. The work caught my fancy; the business of putting on those patterns and trying to stop the thing looking too much like a bone.

"Where's Mary?"

I looked up and there was Talbot looming over me. I saw the line of bright buttons on his tunic and the shape of his head against the sky.

"I don't know, Sarge," I said.

And I didn't. I'd noted where she sat and thought I'd go and talk to her. Then I'd stopped myself for fear of becoming a pest. I wasn't so bothered what the others thought – not any more – but I didn't want to become an annoyance to her. That's why I was whittling away at that branch. I glanced over to the log where she'd been sitting. The emptiness and the great wall of gloom behind it began to alarm me.

"When did you last see her?" Talbot asked.

"Ten minutes ago. A quarter of an hour."

I jumped up and threw my branch aside. He thinned his lips, looking to left and right. He'd made his mind up that she'd gone, I could tell.

"She won't have gone that way," he said with a nod towards the others. "Someone would've seen her. And she won't've headed into the wood. Either she's turned back the way we came or gone off up that brow."

"Why should she do that?"

"I haven't the faintest idea, Hobbs."

"You don't think…"

"What?"

My old doubts came fluttering back like homing pigeons. Was I wrong to trust her? It was like my head was full of flapping, though that might've been the beating of my heart.

"She wouldn't be going to tell … people … about us? Would she, Sarge?"

I prayed that he wouldn't say yes. I didn't want it to be so. I didn't even want to be thinking it.

"She may just be lost, lad. Or maybe a bit confused. That's all."

"We can't leave her, though. Not so close to Black Garlock. We'll have to look for her."

He thought about this for a moment and then lowered his voice.

"Do you want to go?" he said. "To look for her?"

"Yes, sir. I do."

Normally he barked if I called him sir. This time he didn't notice.

"We'll be here for a few hours yet," he said. "Go carefully and make sure you mark the way back. If you lose yourself we won't be able to help you. You'll be on your own."

"Thank you, Sarge."

I slipped off straight away. It didn't occur to me to wonder which way she'd gone. I just ran along by the edge of the wood and up the slope towards the brow of the hill.

* * *

MARY:

It was such a rash thing to do. So wrong and childish. I suppose I wanted to get away from all the lies, and the faces of those men. They haunted me and haunted me and in the end I just ran. If only I'd stopped to think I would have realized you can't do that. You can't run away from such things. You take them with you. It was a long time before I learned that, though.

I kept by the edge of the forest, my cloak wrapped close, and walked and ran, walked and ran towards the top of the hill. It seemed never to come. I looked back once and saw no sign of the camp. They'd built no fire this time. When I did reach the top the land opened out before me like a great carpet. Flat and wide and grey under mist and the thin light of the lifting dawn. In an hour or so I would be able to see for mile after mile. Not just trees and fields but houses too. I was sure there would be houses. Maybe farm buildings and mills. Roads and churches. I longed to see churches.

It didn't seem wise to walk through the middle of this open land so I skirted round to my left, still following the line of the trees, till I came to a track. It came out of the forest and then led down into that broad distance. My heart was glad at the sight of it. A track, wide enough for carts! A sign of people going about their ordinary business. I stepped deliberately into the middle of it and began to walk.

I walked along for ten minutes or more. Hedges

in steep banks rose on either side of me. When I looked through the gaps at the bottom of the hedges I saw the morning mist still hanging in the fields. At times it rolled and swayed a little. I came to an open gate which led into a meadow. In the meadow, blurred by the haze, was a cart.

A large cart with boarded sides.

The sight of it halted me. I stayed there, looking at it and wondering. Then I went up to it, touched the iron rim of the wheels and the worn grain of the boards.

I knew that cart. The picture of it, standing quietly in the stables at the farm, came rushing into my head.

I turned round quickly, almost expecting to see familiar figures walking towards me out of the mist, but the meadow was empty.

What was the cart doing here? And where were Mr and Mrs Campion? And Jonah, and Bridget, and Lizzie? Where were they?

My heart was thumping with both hope and fear. I knew there was nothing I could do but carry on down the track and find what I could there. I knew there was no point tarrying in a deserted meadow. But I couldn't bring myself to leave. I walked slowly round the cart, running my fingers along the sides.

The tailgate was down and resting in the dewy grass. At first I thought there was nothing inside. Just a few blankets left in a heap. Then I saw a foot in a scuffed boot sticking out from under them.

I put my hands to my mouth, stepped back and bumped the tailgate. The wood clacked and chains jangled.

The blankets stirred and someone sat up slowly.

A man with a dark beard.

A stranger.

HOBBS:

I was thinking all sorts as I ran up that hill. Why had she gone? Was it a mistake to choose this way? Maybe she'd tried to get back to the farm. And again, over and over as my feet pounded the earth, why had she gone?

I wore myself out with running and went tumbling onto the grass. For a second or so I lay there with the wet blades brushing the heat of my face. What I saw was the wood. Thick, grey, towering trees, like waiting animals.

I hated the look of them. They didn't care.

I dragged myself up and carried on. Suddenly the land spread out in front of me. A sea of murk and fields. How could I find her in that? It was impossible, though I knew I had to try. I plunged down the incline, cutting straight into the middle with hardly any hope at all.

MARY:

The man knelt, now wide awake. He looked me steadily in the eye and then twisted from side to side to see if I was alone. A small gold chain swung from his waistcoat as he moved. I'd seen it many times before. In the kitchen, at the dining-room table. Mr Campion slipping it through his fingers till his hunter dropped out of his pocket, into his palm. Checking the time with his chin on his chest.

"Where's Mr Campion?" I said.

He took no notice but fixed his gaze on something behind me. I glanced quickly over my shoulder. A second man was walking towards us across the meadow. The remnants of mist swirled round his feet. Tall, striding, a brown scarf tied round his head and across one eye.

"Look at this," the first man said to him angrily when he reached us. "Come at me out of nowhere."

"It's only a girl."

"I could've been knifed in my sleep."

"But you weren't, so what does it matter?"

They both turned to look at me, as if I was an object stuck in their way. I wanted to ask how they had come by the cart but I knew there'd be no point. And I couldn't speak anyway. My voice had dried in my mouth. The man with the scarf lifted his hand. I shrank back but he grabbed my cloak where it fastened at the neck.

"This is all right," he said, jerking back his arm so the cloak came undone. "Has she anything else about her?"

"Is she by herself?" the other said. "That's what we need to know first."

"Don't worry. She's by herself."

He was still holding the cloak in his fist. He

109

pulled it so that it came off my shoulders and sent me spinning against the side of the cart. As I fell I tried to keep moving, to dart away towards the track, but the first man caught me by the hair. Twisting it in his fingers, he forced me into the cart.

"Let's see what we can find," he said. "If she's got nothing we'll think of something else to do with her."

HOBBS:
The first I knew of it was when my eye picked out a small movement somewhere below me and a good way off. I was about halfway down the broad hill. The slope was pitching me forward so fast that I had to stop for fear of tipping myself over again. I stuttered to a halt and slid onto my bum. I took a quick look round before I carried on. I wasn't expecting to see anything. My hopes were very low.

Then I caught sight of that movement. The rest of the place for miles around was still. I squinted my eyes up. It wasn't Mary. I saw that at once.

A man was walking in a field. He moved in a very deliberate way. I only saw him for a second because half the field was hidden by the tops of some bushes. I gave God a little thank you and headed in that direction. I was thinking he might've seen her. It was a poor hope, a bone with no meat, but there was nothing else.

The further I dropped down the hill, the less I could see what was going on, so I had to mark the position of his field in my head. It was down and away to the left. I moved as fast as I could but kept coming up against thick hedges and knots of trees. They sprang up wherever I turned and kept forcing me further and further to the left. Too far.

I'll lose him at this rate, I thought. Let him stop for breath, or trip over his feet. Anything so I can catch him up.

I got forced into a kind of corner where two lines of hedge joined. I can tell you, I said a few bad words then. It looked like I'd have to double back and find some better way. But he'd be gone by then and I couldn't face the thought of that. To be so close and then to chuck it all in. I'd convinced myself the man had seen Mary, you see. I could almost hear him telling me where she went. He was there in my head, smiling and pointing the way. I plunged into the hedge.

I wriggled through that hedge like a mad thing. It did what it damn well could to hold me back; twined its branches into my belt and the folds of my tunic. Then, suddenly, I burst out on the other side, and there I was, standing on a clear piece of track. The backs of my hands were crossed with scratches and there was a sharpness somewhere on my cheek, something gaping and dribbling blood down my chin.

It was a proper track with ruts made by wheels, and I took that for a good sign. The sort of track Mary would take. She wouldn't know who else was on it, though. She wouldn't know who she might run into.

What was she doing out here? I couldn't understand it.

I had to think hard to know which way to turn. I'd gone this way and that so many times I hardly knew where I was pointing any more. Both directions looked wrong to me. But when I cleared my head I saw it was no good going left. That way curved upwards and into the woods.

Almost at once I came to the gate. I saw the cart and a tall man standing beside it. No one else.

To this day I can see that place as keen as anything, though I wasn't there for many minutes. I can see the open gate, the cart, the very shape of the hedges. And sharper than those things I can see that man with his head bound up in some dark cloth. Black marks on the side of his face like he'd been peppered by the blast of a gun.

I called out to him.

He looked over at me. A fierce, startled look. And, oh God, there was something wrong about it. Something that jangled my nerves. Then I heard a muffled scream, someone with their mouth clamped shut, and I knew it was Mary.

I thank the Lord I didn't stop to think. I didn't work it out: I just saw the whole thing, clear as life, and I yelled like mad, running straight into that field, straight for the man.

I think about it now. Many times. I even think how it must've looked to him. The way I came streaking out of nowhere. The uniform of a soldier on my back and smears of blood down my face.

By the saints, I was a wild enough sight.

He was as tall as me but wide and sturdy. He prepared to face me as I came at him. His legs apart, his fists bunched. But I ran full into him before he could do much else. The top of my skull caught his chest and chin. He reeled back and down I went on top of him. He cursed and bucked under my weight.

I clamped myself to him. Our faces rubbed together.

I can feel the scrape of his stubble and the stink from his mouth. Right now I can feel it.

I rocked back and hit him. His head jerked sideways. Breath hissed through his teeth.

Then I turned round, still straddling his body, and found another man at my back. He was already halfway over to me but when he saw me, face to face, he stopped. Just for the blink of an eye. I put my hand to my belt and felt for the bayonet and that was enough. He darted a glance from my face to my hand.

He skipped backwards for a pace or two, swinging his head round like you do when you're looking for someone in a crowd. Maybe he thought there were more soldiers on their way. I don't know. But he ran. Praise His holy name for creating cowards.

All that took only a couple of seconds. Still, it was time enough for the first man to recover and stir himself. I jumped up and stood over him.

God save us but he was a big, brawny creature.

113

I caught sight of the back end of the cart. It was like a bit of fencing made of slats. I stooped to pick it up but it wouldn't come. It was fixed to the cart with long pins. I wrenched the whole bloody thing till it came loose, and then dumped it on him as he was about to get up.

Down he went again with that wooden frame on top of him. I stamped my foot on a cross-piece and trod on it hard. Then fumbled for the bayonet. It whistled out and I leaned over him. His eyes were round and white.

He was scared of me.

Be quick, I thought. If he sees the fear in your heart he'll come at you and the moment will be gone.

I stuck the bayonet through the bars and jabbed him in the arm. The blade went through his sleeve. He squealed like hell.

"Your mate's gone," I said to him. "He's left you. You go too. While you've got the chance."

My voice went all high-pitched. It wouldn't have frightened a lamb. It was the jab of the bayonet that did the job. He nodded madly at me through the wooden bars. I let my foot up and he rolled out.

A blackish patch was growing on his sleeve. He hobbled off, clutching his arm, as if the devil was at his back.

I sometimes wonder if he was. And what it was that came over me.

Suddenly it was quiet and I dropped to my

114

knees. I thought I was going to be sick. Fright and anger and pain went flooding from my head to my belly.

You don't wonder, Talbot had told us. Part of your mind shuts off.

Well, that was true. I found that out. What he hadn't told us was what you feel like when it's over and your mind opens out again.

I toppled onto my hands and spat into the grass. Very slowly I stood up. Before I could take another breath Mary was there. She flung herself on me and nearly sent me over again.

It muddled me. I thought she was filled with anger at me. But it wasn't that. She wrapped her arms tight round my chest, and wept onto my shoulder.

CHAPTER NINE

MARY:
One moment I was sure I was going to die, and the next I knew I was safe. It was a jolt, and that's what started me crying. But once the tears came they were for more than just those moments. I was crying for all sorts of things I'd seen but stayed quiet about till then.

Hobbs held on to me. We were rocking side to side a little, the way you comfort babies. We comforted each other like that because he needed someone holding on to him as much as I did. When I looked up at him his eyes were dazed and his skin was washed out, pale and bloody. There was a deep scratch on one cheekbone.

"He had Mr Campion's watch," I said.

He didn't understand me; didn't know who Mr Campion was, I suppose. He sat down on the grass. Just looking at me as I talked.

"This cart is from the farm. It's the one they

escaped in. Now it's empty. I don't know what's happened."

"Is that why you went off?" he asked. "To find them?"

"No."

"Then why did you go?"

"I … I don't know…"

"You don't know?" His voice lifted, sounding sharp and urgent. "But, Mary, the place is running with soldiers. Theirs and ours."

"I don't think it is. I haven't seen any."

"And we're about to go into battle. Didn't you think of that?"

"I suppose not."

"Not even to wish us well? To say goodbye? Nothing?"

I sat down beside him and took his hand but he pulled it away wearily.

"No," he said faintly. "I'm tired of folk making a fool of me. You said I could write to you and then you ran off. I don't know what's happening any more."

"It wasn't like that, Hobbs."

"Then tell me what it was like, Mary. You were thinking of yourself and not the rest of us. You never meant to have any letter from me. You didn't care."

"Please, don't say that."

"But what am I supposed to say? It seems like I got it all wrong again. I thought you cared but you don't."

"I do, I do."

"How can you?"

"You weren't going to die. I knew you weren't."

"We're on the edge of a bloody battle. What are you talking about?"

"There won't be any battle. Not here."

"But we've been walking for…"

"We've been going the wrong way. I'm not sure where we are but it's nowhere near Black Garlock."

I had to tell him. I couldn't let him think I didn't care. But he shook his head at me in disbelief.

"No," he said. "You wouldn't do that…"

"Not me. Mr Talbot."

"Talbot?"

"He doesn't want you to fight. He took the wrong way when we left the track, ages ago. He's been leading us away from battle, not towards it."

"I don't believe you," he said. "Talbot's a soldier. He's fought before. He wouldn't do that."

"What can I say to you? Can't you see we're lost? Where are these armies?"

"Only a traitor would do that and he isn't a traitor."

"Am I, then? Because someone's led you wrong, Hobbs."

He got up and moved away. Stood there with his head bowed and his back to me.

"He could've killed the lot of us if that's what he wanted," he said without turning round.

"That's just it. He wanted to lead you to safety."

"Safety?"

"Yes."

"We didn't want safety! None of us. We all knew full well we might…"

His voice trailed away.

"Did he know you came to find me?" I asked.

"Yes. He said they'd wait an hour or so and then move on."

"Where to?"

"Black Garlock, I suppose. I don't know."

"Then how could he do that if I wasn't there to show the way?"

"You told him…"

"I didn't tell him because I don't know. He can lead them off because it doesn't matter where they're heading now. Anywhere will do."

A lark went trilling up into the sky. Otherwise there was no sound. It felt as if the whole place was holding itself steady, waiting for something to change.

"You were all getting ready for that battle," I said. "Preparing your minds for it. I couldn't bear to see it."

"So you ran away."

"Yes. I know it was wrong now. But I got so bewildered about things. I couldn't think properly."

All at once he turned round and came back to me. His face was rigid and cold, like I'd never seen it before, much more like a soldier's face.

"I can't think properly either," he said. "I don't

119

know what to make of all this." He waited. "What are you going to do now?"

"I don't know."

"Will you come back with me, then?"

"It's the only thing to do, I suppose."

He turned away from me again and began brushing his tunic down with both hands: brisk movements, not getting him anywhere.

"Right," he said. "Then I'll put it to Talbot and let him speak for himself."

HOBBS:

We kept up a steady pace on the way back, though we were both bone-weary and worn to rags. We didn't speak. There was plenty for me to say but I couldn't trust myself to say it. It was better just to walk.

The sun was just getting up as we drew level with the wood. It skimmed the top of the grass, making shadowy hollows on the long downward slope before us. We were still a long way off when we saw the others. They were slinging on their packs and preparing to leave, but one of them, Kerridge I think, spotted us and waved his arm. Then they just stood there waiting.

We got closer and closer. I looked at Mary to see what signs there were in her expression, but I could see neither good nor bad there. She was dirty and smudged with tears. Even feeling as empty as I did, though, I don't think I ever saw a lovelier face.

There were no greetings for us when we got

down the hill. They could all see that this wasn't a homecoming. I went straight up to Talbot, not even looking at the others.

"I want to know, how far are we from Black Garlock?" I asked.

"You've just come down that hill with our map," he said softly. "Didn't you ask her?"

"I've told him," said Mary.

"Oh? How much?"

"That we're nowhere near. That's all."

"Mary says you knew that, Sergeant. She says this is your idea."

I kept a fast gaze on him, but I could sense the others move about a little, turning their heads to each other. This wasn't what they thought they'd hear from me. Talbot folded his arms and looked back.

"She's right, lad," he said.

"You've brought us the wrong way?"

"I have."

"Why've you done that, then?" I asked. It was a struggle to keep my voice calm. I was feeling the need to shout at someone.

"I've been leading you a dance, Hobbs, but now I'll tell you the truth. It would have to come sooner or later. We've come this way to keep you out of battle."

Then Jack Crowe dropped his rifle and stepped into the ring.

"Did you have orders to do this?" he said. "Are we detailed to take on something else?"

"Nothing else."

"Then we're deserters."

"Oh, Jesus," said Farrar. "They'll shoot us for this."

"You're not deserters," Talbot snapped at him. "If anyone's a deserter it's me. I knew what I was doing."

"But we volunteered," I said clearly. "We're no more than shop folk but we volunteered to fight for our country."

"You don't know what fighting for your country means, lad. I'm sorry."

I'd held myself together till then. Something bad had to come; there was no way round it. Mary or Talbot. Now I knew she was true and he was false. And my heart was hurting in my chest. And my face was twisting up and I started to wail like a little lost kiddie.

CHAPTER
TEN

MARY:
I woke up from a deep sleep and there were voices nearby. The thud of hooves and the jangle of harness. Rumbling wheels. A faint, steady drumbeat that had been going on some time. I was lying on a canvas stretcher set on wooden cross-pieces. When I opened my eyes, I saw the dull yellow of a tent roof, with boxes and sacks piled against it.

The store tent at Black Garlock. The beating sound was not drums but rain.

I swung myself into a sitting position and found that my head was aching. I didn't know how long I'd been there. What day it was, even. I just knew that I'd slept for a long time. When I walked over to the tent flap my limbs were stiff and I felt shaky. I looked out and saw rows of smaller tents and stooped figures running through the rain. Five or six soldiers were lifting saddles from steaming horses. A young man was making his way towards

123

me, stepping carefully over ropes and round puddles. He stopped at my tent and gave a little bow.

"I'm glad you're awake," he said. "They told me to call you an hour ago but I thought you needed to sleep."

He was smiling pleasantly at me, as if I should've known him. I imagined that he was the one who'd brought me to the store tent after we'd arrived. The water was running off his short black hair and down his cheeks. I noticed knots of gold stitching standing out against wet-dark patches on his shoulders. An officer.

He's soaked, I thought slowly; he should come out of the rain. I stepped aside to let him into the tent. He lowered his head as he came in and his boots scraped on the slatted floor.

"It's not up to much," he said, straightening up and glancing round. "But I suppose it's private."

"It's very comfortable, thank you."

"Good, good. There's someone asking to see you."

"What time is it?" I said.

"Four o'clock. Though it's dark enough for night. I'm afraid this rain will make things dreadfully difficult in a day or two."

"Difficult?"

"For the men," he said.

The smile left his face suddenly and he spread his hands and looked down at them. He meant things would be difficult for the battle, but he couldn't bring himself to say the word. Perhaps he thought it would upset me.

"Look," he said, "if you're not feeling quite right yet, I can ask your visitor to wait."

"No. I'm all right. Can you tell me how long I've been here?"

"You came in during the early hours of the morning, just as the rain set in. You were lucky, actually. As far as we can tell, your route took you within half a mile of the enemy lines. Still, you seem to have been in good hands."

"Yes," I said dully. "I think we were."

"Crowe is his name?"

"Yes."

"He's a good man. One of the commercial volunteers, I think, but he has the makings of a fine soldier."

He smiled, bowed again and left.

War turns everything upside down. It was plain to see that he was a young gentleman and I was only a servant. If he'd come to visit the farm I'd've served him tea and he might not even have noticed me. Yet here in this camp he spoke to me as if I was a lady.

It was only when he'd gone, and I began to notice the drumming of the rain again, that I thought about what he'd said.

A visitor. Someone who wanted to see me.

I sat back on the little cot and touched the prickly blanket with my fingers. Once during the night, or some time that morning perhaps, I'd felt that blanket against my face and woken up for a short while. Half-woken, really.

I'd seemed to see his face. As real as if he'd been standing over me.

I think I spoke out loud to him.

He was looking as he did when he got the truth from Mr Talbot. Crumpled with misery. I tried to see him as he really was. To see him smiling. But I couldn't make the picture change and I drifted back to sleep.

After five or six minutes I heard feet splashing outside the tent, and a hand rustling the flap. A broad figure in a high-collared coat was bending in at the opening. Too broad. I knew at once it wasn't him.

"Oh, Mary," said the figure. "It is you."

When he folded down his collar I saw that it was Mr Campion.

HOBBS:

The track between the tents was already churned to mud. It stuck to your boots and your knees. You had to crawl to get in the tent so you couldn't help but bring the stuff with you. And the rain seeped under the canvas. It'd only started spitting when we were half a mile or so from the camp and now everything was like a swamp. A place can change so quickly.

It wasn't rain that kept me awake, though. I was tired enough to sleep through more than that. Maybe I was too tired, I don't know, but my mind bubbled away like a pot full of good vegetables and foul meat.

126

I never knew what was coming to the surface.

I kept seeing my old man standing in the doorway of the shop.

My father was the better man. He had a mean, small mind and treated me like the pots and pans. But he was honest. Once you'd knocked the lie out of Talbot's wall the whole bloody lot came down. You couldn't believe a thing he'd ever told you.

We all thought the same. Even Webster could see the way that man had gulled us. The shame it brought on us. We'd given up all we had to fight for what we believed, to keep our land from the Vixen. I know some of the lads joined because a soldier's life looked better than anything they'd get at home. But that changed. When we came to the battle we were all prepared to do what we could. To lay down our lives.

That was what we had to offer; and Talbot took it away from us.

I think it was because he had no belief. He said he wanted to take us out of the firing line but I don't know. That didn't make sense for a soldier. Even if it was true I couldn't be thankful to him for it.

He was as poor in spirit as a godless heathen. No man ever did a lower deed or fell so far in my thoughts.

Crowe took over. No one decided this but when there were things to say we looked to him. The first thing was work out what to do with Talbot.

"There's not much choice," Crowe said. "Either we leave him here or we take him with us."

127

They to-ed and fro-ed with this for ages. I took no part. I wanted nothing more to do with the man.

"Well, we're still a proper unit," Crowe said in the end. "We have to work to army rules, so maybe we ought to keep him under arrest."

And that's what we did.

Talbot said nothing and made no struggle. He didn't try to argue his way out or fight or run or do anything. There was no guilt or panic in his face. He just took what was coming. Kerridge and Farrar put a round a piece in their rifles and kept them at the ready, but there was no need.

We turned south. No one knew the way to Black Garlock from there but Mary thought that that direction might take us to the main road that went to Motley. Once we found that we'd be able to follow it down till we came to places she knew. And that's the way it turned out.

We walked and walked, never stopping for more than a few minutes at a time. It was a lot easier walking on a wide road. We covered a great distance, half of it in the dark. By the end I was dragging along like some spirit out of his grave. I was that used up.

Mary walked with me. For many a mile I didn't feel like speaking but I was glad she was there. One sure thing in all the turmoil. We began to speak a little to each other as the night came down. Nothing about what had gone on at the cart, and nothing about Talbot. Just things about her farm and my shop; about what she liked and what

I liked. The sort of chat you might have with an old friend. You say what you want and not what you think you ought.

The first we knew that we were going the right way was when we saw the fires. Three or four big camp-fires colouring the sky away to our left. They helped draw us in. Then we could hear horses snorting and calling to each other. It began to drop with rain. Warm, heavy spits to start with.

Three sentries, emerging out of the dark, appeared on the road ahead and challenged us. We didn't have the wit or strength to answer. We stood there looking at them. They shouted again and came forward, cautiously, a step at a time. Then Crowe managed to say something to them.

Things went too fast for me after that. Someone sent for a sergeant. The sergeant sent for officers. And the rain got harder. We stayed where we were and everything happened around us. Each new man spoke first to Talbot. But Talbot would say nothing and Crowe had to keep on explaining. They took Talbot away. A man at each arm.

He was walking away and some horses passed between us. When the horses had gone there was no more sign of him.

Then we were being pushed towards a line of tents. I looked round for Mary. An officer was talking to her. Holding her elbow and leaning over her a little. It looked like they were standing behind a curtain of water. Blurred and wavery.

Someone told me to face front and keep moving.

His voice came to me from the other side of the hissing rain. It was nothing to pay any heed to.

The officer was leading Mary in some other direction, down a different row of tents. I saw her lift an arm and pull up the hood of her cloak. Then she turned round, with her hand still holding the hood, like she was looking for something.

I can see now her pale arm against the cloak and all that dull rain, and against the shadows round her face. And her walking backwards and looking and looking. But I cannot tell – and I could not tell then – whether she sees me or not. There's only shadow where her face should be.

I felt a shove between my shoulders and had to stumble on.

MARY:
He walked up to me and took my hand in both of his and kissed it.

"Oh, Mary," he said, "we thought we'd lost you for ever."

"Is Lizzie safe, Mr Campion?" I asked.

"Elizabeth? Yes, she's safe and happy, poor thing. She doesn't know what all this is about. She thinks it's all a great adventure."

"Is she here?"

"No, no. They're all at Motley. Mrs Campion coping with them all like a saint, and Jonah grumbling about the lazy, wicked ways of towns. But all safe. And if God grants us victory here they'll remain safe."

He sat on the edge of the little cot. He was too bulky for it and his knees were almost tucked under his chin.

"How did you come to be here, Mary?" he asked. "What's happened to you?"

I told him what I could. Not everything: some things were too burdensome to explain. He listened carefully, and nodded his head and sometimes shook it, and watched me all the time I spoke.

"This is a bad business now, Mary," he said when I'd finished the story. "These next two or three days will decide everything for all of us."

"What will happen to me?"

"It's too dangerous to set out for Motley at this stage. Even if we could spare the men to take you. I'm awfully afraid that you must stay here, Mary."

"I want to stay here, Mr Campion."

"It won't be pleasant for you. You'll hear the heavy guns and see the men brought back from the line."

"Then I shall help where I can."

"You'll find it hard. Men will be hurt. Badly hurt. Will you have the stomach for that?"

I thought about Sergeant Talbot's son, Jamie. Imagined him sitting on a chair outside his kitchen door.

"I don't know," I said. "I shall try."

"Good. Try, then, Mary. Yes. And you must pray for us all, too. Paul and I have come to take up arms."

He smiled and opened his heavy coat to show me

the braiding over his tunic pockets.

"They've turned me into an officer. Can you imagine it? It shows how desperate things are, that does. Because I own a patch of good land they think I'm fit to lead men into battle."

Then he told me all that had happened to them since the day they left the farm. How they'd loaded up the cart and waited and waited for me to turn up.

"I've cursed myself many times since," he said. "I feel terrible now that I know we left you in that wood."

"No, Mr Campion. You had all the others to care for."

"Perhaps so. But I can't tell you how glad I am to see you alive and well."

"What happened to the cart?"

"We had to leave the main roads and go by ill-kept backways. The thing was loaded with too much stuff. Pictures and clocks and books. And the axle broke. We had no choice but to abandon it in the end. We did the last stretch on foot, with Mrs Campion and Elizabeth sitting on the horse. It was a lesson to us in greed. We'd piled on more than was good for us."

"But the cart was empty when I found it."

"Yes. Paul came back with me to collect the most precious things. We found those two scavengers picking over the contents, like crows on a dead sheep, and dumping things in a barrow. War gives plenty of opportunities for men like

132

that to feed off misfortune. It's a nasty business.

"There was something of a scrap, I'm afraid. One of them snatched at my coat and got hold of my watch. Then Paul fired off his rabbit gun, to frighten them, and blasted one across the side of his face. They ran off but they must've come creeping back when we'd gone."

He stood up to leave, bending his head to one side to keep it from touching the canvas roof.

"I mustn't tire you," he said. "I'll try to see you again before things come to the boil. But now I think you should get some more rest."

He crossed to the opening and turned to say goodbye.

"Mr Campion," I said. "There's things I have to put in order too. I know time is short but I would be grateful for your help."

"If I can help, Mary, I will," he said.

"I would like to speak to Sergeant Talbot again."

"Talbot? The man who betrayed you, you mean?"

"There's things I have to say to him."

"I don't know. He's under close arrest. But I'll see what I can do."

He smiled and pulled the tent flap aside.

"There's something else," I said quickly. "A young soldier. His name is Hobbs, Arthur Hobbs, and he's one of the commercial volunteers."

"He was with this man Talbot, was he?"

"Yes. I would like to see him one more time, Mr

Campion. He saved my life and … well, I'd just like to say thank you to him."

"Thank you?"

"Yes, Mr Campion. I owe him a thank you."

CHAPTER
ELEVEN

HOBBS:

Permission refused. As simple as that. You can't see her. Shut up. Get back to your tent. Eyes front. Don't waste our time. There's a war on, didn't you know?

"I only want to see that she's all right," I said.

Eyes front. Shut up.

The man I had to ask was some kind of fancy sergeant sitting behind a table in a long tent. He was the straight-backed sort who pulls his hat on so tight you can hardly see his eyes. I'd've got more sense out of a spud. I don't think he understood what I was saying. I asked to see Mary and he jerked his head up as if I'd asked to go straight to the enemy and tell them our plans.

When I pressed on he threatened to put me on a charge.

"Thank you, Sergeant," I said at the end, and snapped him a salute and wheeled round.

"Just a minute, son," he said when I was almost outside. "You were one of those who came in with Sergeant Talbot, weren't you?"

"Yes, Sergeant."

"What do you know about this man Crowe?"

"He's an honest man, Sergeant."

"Well, he's come up with a funny story about Talbot. Doesn't fit the man I know."

"No, Sergeant."

"Just between you and me, son, is there any truth in it?"

"Jack Crowe wouldn't tell a lie. Others might. Others have."

"Well," he said, tapping the table with his fingertips in a thoughtful way. "You'd best get back. It's a sad state of affairs, though. That's all I have to say."

"Yes, Sergeant."

Sad isn't what I'd've called it.

I left and made my way back to the tent. But not directly. I went a roundabout way, thinking I might chance upon Mary. It was a slim chance, I knew. There were tents all over the place and for all manner of purposes.

I came across one stone building. It was a square, made of flint with a slate roof. A shepherd's hut or something of the kind, just high enough for a man to stand up in. Outside were two soldiers with rifles. It looked to me the sort of place they might've found for a girl to be safe in.

I slowed down as I passed and tried to look in. I

could see nothing, though. It had no door but a table had been propped up instead. No sign of a window. I stopped by one of the soldiers.

"What's all this?" I said.

He slid his eyes left and right to make sure no one was walking by.

"Guard house," he said.

"Guarding what?"

"Not what. Who. It's the bloke who ran away."

"Talbot?"

"That's him."

"What'll happen to him?" I asked.

I'd never thought to wonder before. When they led him away and I lost sight of him behind the horses I somehow thought that was the end of the matter.

"Court martial," said the soldier. "You have to do that. Won't take long, I shouldn't think."

"And then...?"

"They'll shoot him."

MARY:
I could see no difference in Sergeant Talbot's face. It looked the same to me, the same as it had been when I'd first seen it. Hard and blank. Eyes that tell you nothing. It was dark in the hut but I could make out those blue eyes, just looking at me, taking things in but giving nothing out. I'm not sure what I wanted to see in them. Perhaps it was blame. Yes, I think I wanted him to blame me somehow.

"They've given me no chairs, Mary," he said.

"No comforts. I can't ask you to sit down."

But I didn't want to sit down. It was awkward to be standing there, so close in that little stone hut, but that's how it should've been anyway. Awkward and difficult.

"I ... I don't know what to call you," I said.

"Call me by my name. Call me Talbot."

That made me think of Hobbs, wanting to keep his other name a secret. These men with their plain names. They don't like you to get near to them. They like to keep things simple, however much of a muddle it all is.

"I asked them if I could see you," I told him. "You see, this is not ... I mean I didn't want things to happen this way."

"No. I didn't want it myself."

"I never thought they'd shut you up like this. I never thought..."

"The rules of war," he said, and I thought he smiled a little. "These are the rules of war. I know them inside out."

"But it's my fault. You could've got away..."

"No, Mary. You mustn't think that. I don't blame you for this."

"But..."

"If there's blame it's right it should fall on me. I tricked you into helping me. I didn't let the men think for themselves."

"Yes, but when I think about ... about Jamie..."

"That doesn't make you change your mind, does it?"

138

"I don't know."

"Jamie was my reason for doing what I did. Every man has his reasons. You have to let people make up their own minds. That's what you told me and I think perhaps you were right."

I didn't say anything to that. I didn't know what to say, or what to think any more.

"I've been chewing all this over," he went on. "It's a hard thing to take in and I'm sure I made a mistake somewhere. I'm not used to that. I was never known for making mistakes. This time, though, I've gone wrong somewhere. Gone wrong in a big way."

"You should've gone when you had the chance. Got away."

"I don't mean that. I didn't plan all this, you know. It only came into my mind after we got lost. Then I began to make up my own rules and live by them. And maybe that was wrong, but I don't think I'd do any different if I had the chance again."

"Then it's not a mistake," I said.

He smiled. Not because he thought I was right. It was a smile to stop me going on at him, and to thank me at the same time. I wasn't expecting it. I wasn't expecting what he said next either. Nor the sudden lightness in his voice.

"You have such fine hair, Mary. Such pretty, fine hair. It's like a candle in this place. And I'm glad you came to see me. To see an ugly old man who's caused you so much bother."

"You mustn't say that, Talbot," I said. Using his

name without meaning to. "I had to come and see you. What will happen next? To you, I mean."

"Court martial. They have to decide what to do with me."

"And what will that be?"

"Oh, they'll make it hard for me, I expect. Like I made things hard for the men. They'll have to. I'd be sorry if they didn't."

"How hard?"

"As hard as the rules allow. But these are military matters, girl. Don't delve into them."

"I want to know. I must know. Will they..."

"Oh," he said and paused and turned away slightly. "I shouldn't think so."

Before I left him he pressed a piece of paper into my hand. A name and an address in a clumsy scrawl.

"Not being sure how things will turn out," he said, "and this being a state of war and everything, I wondered if you'd go and see Jamie and his mother for me. If you get the chance."

"You'd like me to go?" I asked, surprised.

"She's a kind-hearted woman. The best. I know she'd like to see you. I don't like to ask..."

"Of course I'll go," I said firmly.

"It's a fair distance," he added, "but you'll find the way. I know you will."

HOBBS:

They called Crowe and they called Webster, but they didn't bother with the rest of us. I was pacing about waiting for them, treading the grass outside the tent over and over till everything was all mud anyway. I couldn't hear a word that was going on. Every time someone came ducking out of the tent I stopped my pacing and tried to see in. All you could see were the shoulders of the guard and the white head of some officer sitting at the far end. No sign of Talbot.

I'd looked to that man like he was a father and all the time he was cheating and lying and thinking us fools. I was right angry about it and felt like doing some damage. Kicking out. Making someone pay.

But I never thought they'd execute him. I never thought that.

I wanted to have my say and let them know my feelings. I'd worked out the things I'd tell them.

"We joined up to fight for our country and he took that away from us. Yes, he's a liar. Yes, he's a coward. I want no more to do with the man. But I don't want him shot. We'd get liars and cowards and a damn sight worse in and out of the shop, but I wanted none of them shot for it. Punish the man but don't kill him."

It made no sense to me. Why not just put him in the front line when we went out to face the enemy? That wouldn't seem so bad. There might be a point to that. But for his own mates to kill him didn't seem right at all. I knew that they wouldn't listen, though. They weren't interested in what I thought. And, anyway, they didn't call for me.

141

After a bit Crowe came out of the tent and began to walk away. I don't know if he saw me – maybe he didn't – but he headed off with his eyes down like he wanted to see no one. I hurried after him and caught him by the shoulder.

"What's going on in there, Jack?"

"They've heard my evidence," he said. His face was white and serious. "They're just talking."

"What did you say to them?"

"I told them what took place."

He shrugged me off and carried on walking. I let him go and sat down on an old rifle box. I ran my thumb along the line of my boot, thinking all the time, trying to fathom out what I wanted most: justice or mercy. A squidge of mud came off on my thumb and I flicked it back to earth. Both, I thought. I want both.

A corporal marched Webster up to the tent and gave him a little shove. Webster glanced at me before he went in. A puzzled sort of a look, like he didn't know what was expected of him. I gave him a nod and a grin but he didn't respond. He just looked a bit hopeless, kind of afraid that he was the one in the wrong.

I don't suppose he was in there long, though it felt like ages to me. When he came out he sat next to me on the box and looked down at his feet. He said nothing for a good long while. Just looked down, like he was going to be sick.

"They mean to do for him, Hobbs," he said at last.

"I know."

"I tried to tell them about him. He's not a bad man. They muddled me up, though. Everything I said came out wrong. They made me say yes and no and no and yes and they wouldn't let me get it straight."

"Don't worry about it, Webby," I said.

"I can't help it. We don't want him done for, do we, Hobbs?"

"No. We don't."

It was the most I'd ever heard Webster say to anyone.

MARY:

Mr Campion came to see me again, bringing with him a small prayer book. He folded his hands round mine and squeezed them against the book. He didn't stay many minutes and had little to say for himself. I guessed that his mind was on the battle and that he found it hard to concentrate on anything else. Once or twice he looked at me as if he intended to ask me something. Whatever it was, though, he couldn't bring himself to say it.

When he'd gone I took Sergeant Talbot's piece of paper and put it carefully in the prayer book, pressing it like a flower among the psalms at the back.

HOBBS:

That same corporal who'd steered Webster into the court martial came to seek me out. I was puzzled.

It wasn't so I could have my say. I knew it was too late for that.

"I'm like a butler, me," he moaned as we tramped down lines of tents, though he was not unfriendly. "Escorting people here and there. I never thought the army was so keen on showing folk round."

"Where are we off to?" I asked.

"One of the store tents, and don't ask me why because it's not my business to know – or to tell you."

I wish I'd known. I wish I'd known that Mary would be there waiting for me. Then I could've thought ahead and worked it out a bit. I don't know, prepared what I might've said or something.

So there I was, suddenly face to face with her, surrounded by boxes and poles and things, and with no idea what to say. I don't think she knew either, though she'd had time to think. For a while we stood there looking at each other. No sound except the movement of horse and artillery somewhere outside. Very distant. Gentle sounds, they were, jingling away like some child's musical box.

"I owe you a thank you," she said, very serious, and I laughed.

"Are we back to that?" I said. "Thanking and saying sorry turn by turn?"

"I mean it, though. I do want to thank you. Before..."

"Before I go to have my head blown off."

144

It was a right stupid thing to say and I don't know why I said it. I think it was because it was worrying me – the thought of the battle and every-thing – and I wanted to make light of it. I didn't want her to think I was scared and I didn't want her to worry either. But it was a mistake.

"No," I said, and I blushed. "I didn't mean that. I'm sorry…"

And then she laughed. She couldn't help herself, I could tell. She laughed quickly, then looked down and became serious again.

"You mustn't think like that," she said. "I shall pray for your safety. However the battle turns out I shall pray that you'll be all right."

"Then I know I will be."

"Yes. You must believe it. I shall pray so fierce and hard that I know God will hear me."

There was a silence between us. We were stand-ing so close that I thought I could take her hands and make it seem a natural, easy thing to do. So I did. She had such little, white hands. She was a working girl so they weren't soft, but by God they were lovely. To feel them there, resting in my palms – it's a moment I shall never forget.

"And now I feel I should say thank you again," I said, "but I daren't. It'll sound like a tennis match."

I gave her hands a squeeze.

I had a strange thought then. I stopped being afraid. Not that I felt I wouldn't die. It wasn't that. I might very well get myself killed, the same as any other soldier, but it no longer frightened me.

"I must give you something to take with you," she said, and she turned round and suddenly became very busy, moving things and looking about. "That's what they did in the old days. They took some token into battle, given to them by a lady."

"Like knights on horses?"

"Yes. Just like that."

"I'm no knight, Mary. I work in a shop with my dad…"

"It doesn't matter. I'm no lady, either."

She found what she was looking for and turned back to me. It was a little book. It fell open in her hands where she'd marked it with a bit of paper. I could see from the close printing and the way it was set in columns that it was the Bible. Not the whole thing; it wasn't big enough. The prayer book and the psalms.

"This is all I have," she said. "My master, Mr Campion, has given it to me."

Then she did something that shocked me at first. She tore a page out. It didn't seem right. I thought there must be a rule against doing that sort of thing. But it didn't seem altogether wrong either. So I held out my hand and smiled at her.

"Keep this by you," she said, folding the page into a small square. "Think on what it says and think on me."

"I wish I had something to give you, too," I said, and as I said it I thought about my lucky coin. I didn't even know if it was still in my pocket after all we'd been through, but I put my hand to my tunic and it was. "It's not worth a thing," I said, "but it might do to remind you."

I had no chance to say another thing because the corporal flapped open the tent just then. His head came in, looking very big all of a sudden, and he gave a loud cough.

"We're on our way back now," he said.

That was the way of our meetings. They never got the chance to end properly. The army was always stepping in.

I expected the corporal to jibe me as we walked back through the rows of tents. To have a dig at me for spending those few minutes in a store tent with a lass. And I would've given him answer for answer. I didn't care. He said not a word, though. The hours before a battle do strange things to a man. I'd found that out already.

When I got back to the tent I shared with Kerridge and Webster, I dropped down on to my bed roll without a word. I unfolded that torn page and looked at it. There wasn't much light and I had to hold it close to my eyes.

"What you got there?" I heard Kerridge say. He was watching me from his own bed, with his hands cupped round the back of his head.

"I've been to see Mary," I said. I wasn't going to tell him a lie. Not at a time like that. "She's given me something to take with me when the battle begins."

"Lucky man," he said.

He wasn't joking this time. He smiled for a moment and then turned himself away so I could read it in peace.

I'm not much of a reader and, what with the light being so poor, it took me a little while to work it out. Psalm 46, it was.

God is our refuge and strength, a very present help in trouble. Therefore will not we fear, though the earth be removed, and though the mountains be carried into the midst of the sea.

A very present help. I'd heard the words before, in church, and they'd gone straight past me. This time they stuck. A very present help. It may be a bad thing to say – I don't know – but I thought of Mary as my present help before I thought of the Lord. Mind you, I thought of the Lord as well. I thought of Him as hard as I'd ever done in my life. And He was there all right. It's just that Mary was more clear.

She must've had it in mind to give me that particular psalm, because she'd written her own words in the little space at the bottom.

"From Mary," she'd written. "With love."

MARY:
There was no chance of seeing him when the army marched out. So many soldiers, all kitted out the same, all moving in the same steady way, but with

148

different faces. When you see so many men together in one great crowd it amazes you that all those faces can be so different. You'd think they'd merge into one but they don't. Wave after wave went by and I didn't see one face that I recognized. At one point I saw in the distance a man in a heavy coat whirling his horse round, trying to turn it the right way. I thought it was Mr Campion but it wasn't.

The dull thump of boots on the earth filled my ears. The clanking of metal and the rattle of drums. Thin voices calling out orders over the mass of bobbing heads. Sounding so bright and cheerful. And the tinny sound of pipes. Like it was some great dance.

And all their faces so set and firm. After a while I couldn't stand and watch any more. I couldn't bear the thought of what they were going to; wondering which of those faces would come back and which would end up in the mud.

And I stopped looking out for him. Suddenly, I didn't want to remember him like that; one set expression in a crowd of others. I wanted to remember his face as I'd seen it in the store tent. The look he gave me when I handed him the page from my prayer book and he gave me his coin. Him laughing a little when we exchanged sorries and thank yous.

I turned my back on it all. I went as far away as I could get – under the shelter of a small blackthorn at the rear of the camp – and I prayed my prayers as fiercely as I could, with the coin squeezed tight in my hand. The marching and the little voices shouting orders, the pipes and the drums I could not shut out. They were there all the time I held on to the tree and prayed.

For old Mr Campion and Paul.

For the soul of Sergeant Talbot, who could be no part of it.

And for him. A shop boy dressed up as a soldier. Over and over for him.

CHAPTER TWELVE

MARY:

The sergeant was right: I found the place without much trouble. A cottage in a dip in the land, set back from a dusty road. A hill rose gently to the skyline above the cottage. Dotted over it were a few cows. The grass was deep green and looked soft because it was so long.

It was late in the day and towards the end of summer when I arrived. The cottage looked so peaceful. If my heart had been less heavy I might've found it a comfort. I might've been soothed by it. But I don't think I wanted that.

"People are kind," Mrs Talbot said, showing me through a narrow corridor to the kitchen. "You're kind to come all this way."

She had large eyes and hands that were always busy. She wasn't as tall as I'd imagined her to be and she had copper hair, parted in the middle and pulled back tight so that it shone.

"It's not so kind," I said. "I wanted to come."

"Well, it means a lot to me. To both of us. To think that people come out of their way to visit us. All sorts."

We spoke only a little of Sergeant Talbot to begin with. I thought it wrong to say too much. Perhaps if she'd asked I'd've said more but she seemed content with the few things I wanted to tell her. I explained a little about how I came to know her husband. I told her what I could see she knew: that he was a good man, someone to be proud of, and that his men were devoted to him. I said two or three times that I was sorry but I made no mention of the circumstances of his death. To this day I don't know how much she'd heard about all that.

"Will you come and say hallo to Jamie?" she said, smiling a little.

"I would like to. I promised that I would."

"He likes to sit in the garden at the back on these warm evenings."

We found him on an old bench, his back to us, apparently staring up at the hills. He sat very upright and his pale, ginger hair had been neatly combed. I guessed she'd done it for him.

"Jamie," said Mrs Talbot. "There's someone to say hallo to you. Someone known to Daddy."

As we moved in front of him, I saw his arm, with the sleeve folded and pinned where his hand should have been. It rested in his lap.

"Hallo, Jamie," I said.

He turned his face to us but didn't speak. It was

an open, trusting face, such as you see on small children sometimes.

"I met your father, Jamie. He wanted me to come and say hallo. He wanted me to say how much he cared about you…"

He made no answer and I couldn't think what else to say. He tilted his head up to me. A good-looking boy. He squinted a bit in the sun and he might've been smiling. I wanted it to be so but I couldn't be sure.

"Come in and have some tea," Mrs Talbot said and we turned away and left him sitting in the garden.

She pushed a few sticks onto the kitchen fire and hung a small black kettle over it. She seemed more at ease when she was occupied like this.

"It's a blessing we can all sleep safe in our beds now," she said. "A terrible time it was but we have that blessing in the end."

"Yes."

"You say you were there? At Black Garlock?"

"Yes. I helped with the men who were wounded."

The way I said it made it all sound so clean and easy. Just another job to be done. I couldn't put it any other way, though. It was far beyond me to find the words for everything that happened all those days ago.

She came and sat beside me at the kitchen table, looking at me carefully for several moments.

"You didn't say your name," she said.

153

"It's Mary."

"Ah, yes."

She nodded, as if she knew; as if she'd been expecting me. Not just another visitor, but a girl called Mary. For a second I wondered if Sergeant Talbot had written to her about me. I wondered if she knew of my promise and had been waiting for me to keep it.

"It's a hard answer to a hard question, is war," she said at last. "There'll have been such a lot of muddle and chaos. And people lose so much."

"Oh yes," I said. "They lose so much."

I remembered standing still for a moment with chaos all around me.

It was a considerable while after the battle had started but you couldn't tell how long exactly because time was running its own course. A rag of bloodied shirt was hanging from my hand and there was a roaring in my ears I couldn't understand.

A while ago I'd seen my first dead soldier. One of the surgeons had bundled him to the side of the tent and left him there because there were wounded men screaming out for help. The dead soldier had thick grey hair and his jaw had fallen open, giving him a kind of shocked look. My first dead soldier. But I couldn't stop to take it in. A while later I lost count of all the dead I'd seen.

Then I stopped running; stopped helping. Just stood still while it all happened around me.

There were soldiers hurrying in all directions. Stretchers being carried from place to place. The guns thumping in the distance. And I just stopped. It was like being in the middle of a whirling circle. I was still and the world was whirling round me. Like the dances Mr Campion held in the yard at harvest. The point comes when you're at the centre and all the other dancers are chasing round and round you and it's your turn to be at the hub of it all.

A dance. A game.

I remembered Sergeant Talbot saying that war was a game.

But here you couldn't tell who'd won and who'd lost. And winning and losing didn't seem to matter much.

I don't know how long I stood there letting it all happen. It couldn't have been very long. Eventually someone shouted at me and I joined in again. I took a beaker of water from the grasp of a dead man and handed it to one who was still dying.

Darkness came and with it raw, orange fires and pale lamplight inside the tents. Then morning followed. I heard the pitter of rain on the canvas and knew that the battle was either coming to a stop or moving away.

It was only then – with the soft sound of that rain – that I realized I'd seen no one I knew. None of the faces I'd looked for when the wounded were first brought in. I walked out of the tent and came to a carriage with a broken shaft. I curled up in the shelter of it and went to sleep with talking and shouting and crying still in my ears. And still not knowing.

The kettle was spouting steam in the fireplace. Mrs Talbot stood and attended to it. She set the teapot on the table and crossed to the open door, her arms folded, staring out.

"You have to start again," she said. "You count your losses and see what God's left you, and then you start again."

"It can't be the same, though, Mrs Talbot. It can't ever be the same."

I knew she'd understand more about that than me, but I said it all the same.

"No. Nothing like the same. I still have Jamie and that's a blessing. But..."

Her voice trailed away and she turned her back on the door. She came to sit beside me again.

"I've lost a husband," she said. "Before that I lost a brother." And then, leaning a little closer, "You've lost people, too, Mary."

"Yes."

"And a home? Do you have a home?"

"Oh, yes. Mr Campion, my master, he was spared. I look after his little daughter and I have a good room in the attic and..."

I stopped myself talking. I wanted to cry just then but it wouldn't have been right to, not in front of her when she'd lost so much.

"She's a poppet, my little Lizzie," I said as

brightly as I could. "I could bring her to see you one day."

"I'd like that."

"It would be an adventure for her, and I'm sure Mrs Campion would say yes."

We sat for a while and had tea and some bread. At one point she stopped talking and leaned across the table. She took the little chain I wore round my neck and held it in her fingers, frowning at it.

"A strange thing to be wearing, Mary," she said. "The Vixen's image."

"I don't wear it for the Vixen," I told her.

She let go of the chain and, though she looked as if she would say more, remained silent. Then she sighed and went on, asking further questions which I answered where I could. I told her a little more about Sergeant Talbot and about the others. Told her their names. There was one name I didn't mention because I didn't trust myself to say it out loud. She watched me, and listened, and nodded. Then she said:

"I'm a canny old lady, Mary. I like to find out what I can about people who come to see me."

"I'll tell you all I can, Mrs Talbot."

"It's not what you tell me. It's what I see for myself."

"What do you see, then?" I asked, looking at her uncertainly.

"Well, I see that you tell the truth. You've come because you promised Talbot. You've come to see Jamie and me. Not for any other reason."

157

"What other reason could there be?"

"I thought for a spell that you'd just come looking."

"Looking?"

"People do. As I said, there's so much gets lost in war. I thought you might've come looking for what you've lost."

"I've looked and looked for that," I said after thinking for a while. "But it's not why I'm here today."

She began to take the tea things to the sink, busying herself and brisk all of a sudden.

"You've given it up, have you?" she asked.

"No. I shan't ever give it up. Not till I know. And then I shan't give up thinking."

She spoke as if she knew what it was I was keeping inside me, as if we had an understanding.

"There's other visitors we sometimes get," she said. "I was going to say when you came in but I wanted to talk a bit first. To see what I could see."

"What other visitors?"

"Two lads back from the war. Two lads who knew Talbot."

"And came to find you?"

"Came to bring me word, like you did. And more."

"What more, Mrs Talbot?"

"Looking for something. For different things. That's what you get after battles. People looking for things they've lost."

She was at the sink with her back to me. I was

watching her carefully but I couldn't tell what she was thinking. And another question had come to my mind but I didn't dare to ask it.

"Now I've talked with you for a bit I find they're known to you as well," she said. "At least, one's known to you. Little man with spectacles. Not a lad, really; getting on in years."

"Jack Crowe."

"That's right. He had a lot on his mind when he fetched up here. Had all sorts to tell me about Talbot. Wanted me to know what a good man my husband was. I told him I knew that and he seemed pleased. I think that's maybe what he'd been looking for."

She turned to face me, a dark shape against the window. She took a cloth and wiped her hands.

"He stayed a day or two and then went on his way," she said. "But the other one ... I don't know. You made no mention of him when you were telling me."

"No. I..."

"It could be you don't know him, of course."

"Where did they go?"

"Jack had a family to get back to. The other lad stayed behind."

She paused and I could feel her looking at me.

"Said he'd lend me a hand about the place. Said he was waiting."

"Waiting?"

"Though he wouldn't say what for. Asked if I'd mind him waiting here for a spell. And he's a good lad. Talks to Jamie and helps with our few cows."

She moved over to the kitchen door and looked out. I followed her gaze, over the corner of the garden to the hill in the distance.

"He's on his way back now," Mrs Talbot said, so quietly I could hardly hear her. "I think I'll sit with Jamie a while. You rest there, Mary. As long as you like. You just sit and wait."

She smiled and went into the garden without looking back at me. I stood slowly and spread my fingers on the table to steady myself. I looked out of the door and beyond to the distant slope.

Five or six slow cows were walking heavily homewards, and behind them a tall figure was swishing a stick through the air as he made his way down the hill through the long grass.